C000064037

STARVATION LAKE

A DCI SEAN BRACKEN NOVEL

JOHN CARSON

MAX DOYLE SERIES
Final Steps
Code Red
The October Project

SCOTT MARSHALL SERIES

Old Habits

STARVATION LAKE

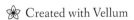 Created with Vellum

To Kara Page, with many thanks.

ONE

Andrea Harrison always said she would rather live a fun life and die young than live to a ripe old age.

She was going to get her wish.

Andrea's idea of fun was going dancing, having a few drinks with friends and going somewhere hot for a holiday. It was not meeting her new boyfriend on a smelly old farm in the middle of nowhere. Despite him telling her she was going to experience a once-in-a-life-time event.

She parked her car in the little car park off to one side and held her mobile phone in one hand, trying to decide whether she was going to call her friend Maxine or not, to let her know where she was. It was their buddy system, if one of them was going out with some-body new.

'Come on, Andrea, make a decision,' she told

herself. She should have looked at her horoscope that morning. Maybe the stars would have given her guidance.

Peter was married, but he was in a loveless marriage. He was a few years older than she was. Not old enough to be her dad, but more mature. They hadn't been going out for long, but that didn't matter; he was fun and she didn't want a long-term relationship with him. She knew Maxine wouldn't approve, so now Andrea was holding her phone, indecision weighing her down.

She held back while she looked around her.

Peter had said it was going to be a surprise, but now she thought she could guess the surprise: he was going to tell her he had bought this place for them.

The For Sale signs were everywhere.

That punched her in the gut. She didn't want to settle down with him. Was that what he was planning on telling her tonight? That he was leaving his wife? She should make it clear that she only wanted to have fun, not grow old with him.

No, it was time to call Maxine, be straight up with her and tell her she was available for a drink after all. Peter could shove this dump up his –

There was a knock on her window. She screamed and jumped back. Then she saw who it was and rolled her window down.

'Peter! You scared the crap out of me.'

'Hi, honey, I missed you too.' He smiled at her and leaned down, poking his head in for a kiss, like he couldn't wait two minutes for her to get out of the car.

'Jesus, you gave me a fright,' she said.

'Sorry. I thought you'd seen my car coming in.'

Andrea looked around and didn't see any other car. 'Where's your car?'

'Round by the house. I didn't see you, so I came looking for you. This is where the farm vehicles parked. Come on, let me show you around.'

She squeezed the phone. It wasn't too late to make a call.

'Coming,' she said, and waited until he moved out of the window. That was one of the things about Peter: he could be annoying. Like a papercut.

He laughed and stood back, watching her struggle across the rough car park in her stilettos without offering her a hand. There was a coating of snow on the ground, making it slippery.

Annoying.

'You sure know how to spoil a lady,' she said.

He held up his hands. The smile was still there. Maybe he'd had plastic surgery and couldn't do anything *but* smile now.

'I wanted to show you this place because a client of

mine has just bought it and I'm in line to get a pretty big bonus.'

She felt relief wash over her like an incoming wave. Thank Christ for that. This annoying little man didn't want her to be his missus and stay in the farmhouse wearing an apron all day.

He laughed again, like he was telling himself jokes and she wasn't privy to the punchlines.

Maybe the punchline she was going to deliver later would wipe the smile off his face. This relationship was getting less fun by the minute.

'I know who's bought the farm, and he's going to build flats and houses on the land.'

'It's hard to imagine why anybody would like to stay out here,' she said, turning her nose up at the smell as he slid open a large steel door.

'Edinburgh is getting more and more expensive, so people are moving out of town. This location is perfect: not too far from the city centre, but a beautiful area to live in. It's perfect. And you know what's best?'

'No, do tell.' She made a face as the smell got stronger. She was expecting a cow to come storming out of the brick building at any moment.

'I told my wife I'm leaving her. For you.' He beamed at her and held his hands out wide.

'You did what?' she said, starting to feel cold. It seemed the wind was done playing at the ski centre for the day and was now coming off the hills to chill her to the bone.

Or was it just Peter's words that were doing that?

'She got pissed-off and started throwing things. Smashed the fucking TV, but I don't care. She can have the house. I'll find a place until our dream house is built here. You can move in and we can stop sneaking around. This building project is going to get off the ground in the next few months, and this time next year, we'll be in a big four-bedroom. A room each for Annie and Paul.'

'Who're Annie and Paul?'

'You see what I did there? I gave our kids the same initials as us. Isn't it exciting?'

'Wait...what?'

His smile slipped for a second. 'Aren't you happy? Isn't this what we talked about?'

Her hand was inside her jacket pocket, still holding on to her phone; she willed it to ring. This was going way faster than she'd thought it would, and she hadn't thought the nut-ball would actually leave his wife.

'Look, Peter, don't you think we're rushing things?'

'What do you mean? I don't think for one second that we're rushing things. I'm in love with you, Andrea.'

'We barely know each other, Peter.'

'I know, but sometimes you just have a feeling. I get that with you, more than I did with my wife.'

She had to admit, she enjoyed being taken to expensive restaurants, being given little trinkets made of real gold, sipping champagne, but everything had a price. And the cost of those things was moving in with this moron.

'Look, sweetheart, I know that you love me, but things are maybe moving too fast for me. I hope you understand.'

He didn't seem to understand – he just went into the old cowshed. Had he heard her words, or was he just tuning her out? Was he now inside the manky old building crying like a boy?

'Peter, come out and talk to me.' She stood shivering in the cold. Maybe she should just go back to her car and drive off.

'Peter, honey, come out of there.' Nothing. Not even a squeak from him. Sulky little bastard.

She walked across the dirt track to the sliding door and looked in. There was nothing there but the smell, and some hay near the front. Or was it straw? She could never tell the difference.

'Peter, I'm leaving now. Congrats on...whatever this is, but just stay with your wife.'

'Oh, God, I think I've broken my ankle,' she heard him say from further inside.

'What?' *See? Annoying,* she said to herself. Only this clown could go into an old cow's toilet and break a fucking ankle. God, she couldn't imagine him with kids.

This had made her mind up; there was no way she was going any further with this relationship. She would drive him to the hospital if necessary, drop him off; then she could give him his own chapter in her book of memoirs one day.

'Peter, where are you? I can't even see you.' She turned on her phone's little light and shone it inside the door. Then she moved in, her light bouncing off the walls and the hay on the floor.

'I'm over here. Near the back. Oh, God, I can't even stand on it,' he said.

'I'm coming,' Andrea said, her voice lined with displeasure now. 'And you're going to buy me a new pair of fucking shoes,' she said in a lower voice.

No response.

'Peter, keep talking to me, for God's sake,' she said, all pretence of liking him now gone. 'Where are you?'

'Right here,' he said from behind her.

She turned to face him, about to give him a piece of her mind, but screamed instead.

The man was dressed in an old apron. A gas mask sat on top of his head. He pulled it down over his face with one hand, bringing the knife down with the other.

TWO

She was a day late with the death threats.

The seventeenth day of December had come and gone and the serial killer whom DCI Sean Bracken had put away six years ago was late with her phone call. Now the clock had ticked over into the eighteenth of December, it was ten hours into the day and she still hadn't called.

Bracken had never thought he'd miss receiving a call from a killer, but he did. He'd been looking forward to this one. It was a dance routine they went through. She would call him and tell him that one day they'd be face to face again and she would kill him. Then he would get to gloat, and he'd end the call by telling her he'd speak to her next year.

This year she was late.

The traffic coming over from Fife into Edinburgh was still busy when every decent office worker should have been at their desk an hour ago, he thought as Corstorphine came up to him in a flash. It had been a while since Edinburgh beckoned, and although coming here hadn't been his first choice, it made his daughter happy.

He saw the sign for the guest house on St John's Road and indicated, cutting off a cyclist dressed as Santa as he pulled into the driveway. The cyclist stopped and dismounted as Bracken parked the car in the car park, which might have been a garden at one time.

'Oy! What the bloody hell are you doing?' the cyclist shouted. Then he saw the big man getting out of the car.

'Sorry, pal!' Bracken shouted. 'Merry Christmas.'

The man kept walking up the driveway. Bracken took out his warrant card and held it in front of him. 'Polis. The next move is all on you, son. You can get back on your bike, or I can give you a Christmas you'll never forget.'

The man decided the better part of valour was to get back on his bike. 'Fuck you!' he shouted and stuck two fingers up as he rode away.

Bracken took his bags from the boot of the car and

checked his phone once more. Why did he feel disappointment? Ailsa Connolly was in the right place, locked up in a psych ward. She wouldn't be getting out anytime soon. Still, it smarted.

At the doorway waiting for him was his old friend DI Bob Long. Or as he was known these days, Bob Long. Retirement had robbed him of the DI.

He smiled at Bracken. 'What's next? The tooth fairy telling you to go fuck yourself?'

'There's a first time for everything,' Bracken replied, smiling. He looked at the sign above the door; Glenfiddich Hotel. 'Named after one of Scotland's finest whiskies, I see.'

'Mary and I were thinking of names when we bought this place. I happened to pour myself one, and the rest is history.'

'Just as well you weren't drinking Buckfast.'

'If it had been the day before...well, say no more. It's good to see you again, Sean.'

'Likewise, my friend.'

'I don't have to salute you now, do I?' Bob said, grinning. 'You made DCI. Good man.'

'We'll see. Maybe you can polish my boots if I leave them outside my door at night.'

Bob looked unsure for a moment.

'I'm kidding, Bob. I'll just wipe them on the duvet.'

Bob laughed. 'Come away through to the back. Leave your bags there.'

Bracken left his bags where nobody would trip on them and followed his friend back through to the private part of the house. They entered the living room.

'Mary, look who's here,' Bob said as if he'd just let Santa Claus into the house.

'Hello, Mary,' Bracken said, holding out his hand for a shake, but Mary went in for a hug.

'Handshake indeed, Sean Bracken.' She stood back and smiled at him. 'It's been a long time. You never come to visit us anymore.'

'You know how it is: work.'

'Aye, I do that,' Bob said.

'No, I don't know how that is,' Mary said. 'You went to work in Fife, not on Mars. A hop, skip and a jump away.'

'Leave the laddie alone,' Bob said, and Bracken was surprised by the term. He knew Bob Long had recently turned fifty, but he was only five years older than Bracken.

'I missed him, that's all. I haven't seen him since the New Year's party last year. Remember the nights out we had with...' Mary stopped herself, remembering that Bracken had divorced the fourth member of their Saturday night quartet.

'Catherine. Yes, I remember,' said Bracken. 'But I want you to be able to talk about her, if you like. Just because we're divorced, doesn't mean we didn't have good times. If it's any consolation, she still likes you two. She knows I'm coming to live here until I get a place sorted. I gave her a heads-up.'

'Anyway, love,' Mary said, 'come and get a nice cup of coffee. I was about to put the kettle on. Bob, go and put the kettle on.'

Bob trudged off to the kitchen, admitting defeat in the war of who wore the trousers in the house.

'Take your coat off, Sean. Nobody'll nick it. The charity shops aren't open yet. And God knows there are enough in Corstorphine.'

'Cheap paperbacks, though. You know I'm a tight wad who likes to save a few notes.'

'You got any plans for Christmas?' she asked Bracken as they followed Bob into the kitchen. She hung his coat up.

'I'm hoping to see Sarah. She's in a flat up in Marchmont with a group of student friends.' Sarah, his little girl – not quite little anymore.

'If you've not been invited anywhere else by then,' said Mary, 'you're welcome to have dinner here with us. I'll be cooking turkey for some of our permanent guests. Christmas Day is only a week away.'

'Smashing. I'm not sure how the rental market will

be this time of year. I didn't snag anything before it was time to start the new job.'

'Don't worry. You can stay here as long as it takes.' She smiled at him and a quick look passed between them, maybe Mary thinking of what might have been.

Bob flicked the kettle switch. 'Make yourself at home. Don't worry about your coat; the charity shops aren't open yet.'

'I already said that,' Mary said to her husband's back.

'Some things are worth repeating.'

'That doesn't include your jokes.'

Bob chuckled and made the coffees while Bracken sat at the kitchen table.

'Did she call you?' Bob said.

Bracken was silent for a moment. 'No.'

'Jesus. That's the first time in...what...six years?'

'Yes. Six times she's called, the first time on her first day in Carstairs. This would have been number seven, but nothing.'

'They should never have moved her into her own ward in the Royal Edinburgh. I would have left her in Carstairs.' Bob's face took on a darker look.

'She wouldn't have led us to the sixth victim, Bob,' Bracken said. 'She told us where her last victim was buried so she could get a move to the new Royal Edinburgh. It was all politics.'

'Maybe wedded bliss has taken precedence,' Mary said.

Both men looked puzzled.

'What do you mean?' Bracken said, breaking the silence.

'Didn't you know?' Mary said. 'She got married last Saturday.'

THREE

During his twenty-odd years on the force, Sean Bracken had seen his fair share of the horrendous things that some people did to others. Monsters in human form. One who stood out was Ailsa Connolly, a woman who could hold an intelligent conversation, play a terrific game of chess or rip your throat open with a blunt saw and then take your eyes. Although the weapons of choice had been different in each of the six cases. The last one had involved a pair of tin snips which had been very effective in removing different parts of the man's anatomy.

Bracken wondered just how long she would have continued her reign of terror had he not figured out she was behind the killings.

On one hand, he had been the man of the hour back then, a hero in the eyes of the press, who gave him his fifteen minutes of fame. On the other hand, they would have burned him at the stake if they could have got away with it.

How could you not know? was the question on everybody's lips. It was an undercover job, but the press didn't want to hear about it.

Still, he had caught her, and saved a victim in the process, so he was given kudos for that. He'd been a celebrity of sorts but had always taken the opportunity to remind people that five families were still hurting because of Ailsa Connolly. His own family would have been hurting had she carried out her plan.

Then came the phone call, a year after she was taken into the hospital.

When she told him where he could find the body of victim number six.

A man found buried in a farm in Perthshire.

Now there were six families hurting.

Bracken had applied to Fife Constabulary after that. It was a move he'd been thinking about for a long time anyway. The promotion had come a couple of years later.

A knock at his bedroom door snapped him out of his thoughts.

'Come in,' he shouted.

Mary popped her head round the door. 'I change

the sheets a few times a week,' she said to Bracken. 'Those were fresh on this morning.'

'Thanks.'

She walked in and closed the door behind her. 'Bob's so glad you came here to stay.'

'How's he doing?'

'Oh, you know.' Her smile was tinged with sadness. 'He puts a brave face on it.'

'Not every copper would have done what he did.'

'I know that, Sean. If the floor hadn't collapsed, then he would have died in the fire with those kids.' She said it out loud, but it was meant for her own benefit. Something she would tell people if they ever asked why Bob was pensioned out of the force on medical disability.

He'd run into a burning house to save two children who were trapped upstairs, without once thinking about his own safety. The floor had collapsed, and he'd kept hold of the kids. The little boys being dead didn't take anything away from his brave act.

'He's lucky he isn't in a wheelchair.'

'Aye, he is that.'

Mary looked at Bracken for a moment like she was about to cry, but she smiled again.

'I serve dinner at six and breakfast from seven until nine. I don't have a full house. You'll meet the others tonight. Mr and Mrs Clark are in the room next to yours. Nice old couple. You'll meet Natalie too. She's nice. You'll like her.'

Bracken stood up and went over to her and put his hands on her arms. 'Are you sure he's okay with me being here? Bob, I mean.'

'What? Of course he is. To be honest, I think he's looking forward to having a wee bit of banter with you. I try, but it's hard. Sometimes he likes to talk about the old days on the force.'

Bracken took his hands away and smiled. 'He and I can have a wee dram later tonight then. Reminisce.'

'Thank you, Sean.' She kissed him on the cheek, her lips staying a little bit too long. He watched her leave.

He had just filled the drawers with his clothes when his mobile phone rang.

'I'm looking for DCI Bracken,' a voice said.

'Then you've found him.'

'I'm your DI, sir, DI Jim Sullivan. We got a shout and I thought you'd want in on this.'

'What's it about?'

'A woman was found dead in a barn past Fairmilehead. No eyes.'

'Give me the address. I'll be right there.'

He scribbled it down on a notepad and put his jacket on. *No eyes.*

Just like Ailsa Connolly's victims.

18

FOUR

It had been a while since Bracken had been near the Hillend ski slope, but he had been born in Edinburgh, so he still knew his way about. The Pentlands were sugar-coated. Or that's what he used to tell his daughter when she was little. Now they just looked stark and cold as he hit the A702 Biggar Road.

Snow was starting to come down again, adding to the piles at the side of the road. The slick conditions didn't seem to bother some motorists, who only slowed down for the police cars at the side of the road further on, before speeding up again.

Bracken pulled into the farm entrance off the main road, past some For Sale signs, and saw a younger man with a fashionable overcoat and a neatly trimmed beard standing talking to a young woman. He parked outside a low brick building and got out.

'DCI Bracken?' the man said, approaching the car.

'I am that. And you are?'

'DI Sullivan. Jimmy if you like.'

He held out his hand. Bracken wasn't sure yet if he liked the guy, but he shook the proffered hand anyway.

'This is DS Ishita Khan. We call her Izzie.'

'Pleased to meet you, sir.'

Bracken shook her hand. 'And what will you be calling me?' he said.

'I think we should be fine with *sir*.' Sullivan looked at Izzie as if for confirmation, and she nodded, like they'd been rehearsing meeting the new boss.

'I meant behind my back.'

'That would be telling,' Sullivan said, not missing a beat.

'Tell me what we have,' Bracken said, watching the cold air snatch his breath away.

Sullivan turned and pointed towards the small car park off to one side. A uniform was standing at its entrance, guarding the police tape that was stretched across it.

'A car was parked in there when the estate agent turned up to meet a prospective buyer. He saw the door to this barn was open and thought the client was here already. He went in and found the girl lying on some old hay. Then he called us.'

My first day in Edinburgh and we have a murdered

woman with her eyes out, Bracken thought. This wasn't the kind of start he'd expected. His idea of a first day back was sitting in the office, shuffling paperwork, drinking coffee and getting to know the others. Now he was out in the land that time forgot, hoping he wasn't going to get his boots covered in some kind of muck that an animal had left behind.

'Pathologist here?' he asked, his boots crunching the snow as they walked towards the barn.

'Aye. She's in there with the victim. Forensics are here too.'

Bracken indicated for Sullivan to lead the way and they stepped out of the wind and put shoe covers on.

'Aw, shite,' a young man said, leaning over, his hand in a pile of something. He struggled to stand up straight. When he did, his hand was covered in cow shit.

'That's DC Charlie Nelson,' Sullivan said. 'This is the new boss, DCI Bracken.'

Nelson held out a hand for the boss to shake.

'Oh, I don't think so, son,' Bracken said. 'I've shaken some manky hands in my time, but no' one that's covered in cow shite.'

'This was an old cowshed, apparently,' Sullivan said before Bracken could ask.

'What gave it away?' Bracken said. 'The fact it doesn't smell like expensive perfume?'

Nelson grinned at Sullivan.

'Go and wash your hands, Charlie,' Sullivan said, dismissing the younger man.

A woman turned to look at them. 'This the newcomer you were telling me about?' she said to Sullivan. She looked to be in her forties, with blonde hair tied back into a ponytail.

'This is DCI Bracken. Sir, Dr Pamela Green.'

'Call me Sean,' he said, shaking the doctor's hand.

'Dr Green.'

Christ, I should have gone with the title thing first, Bracken thought. Then the pathologist broke into a wide smile.

'I'm kidding; call me Pam,' she said, letting his hand go. 'This is one of the mortuary techs, Chaz.'

Chaz smiled at him. A young woman with dark hair, also pulled back. She was slim but looked like she fought hard to keep it that way.

'Okay. What are we looking at here, Pam?' His eyes flitted past her to the form of a female lying on the ground.

'Her ID says she's twenty-nine and not from around here.'

'Where's she from?'

'Dunfermline. Her name is Andrea Harrison.'

'Do you know the cause of death?'

Pamela nodded. 'I'm fairly certain, but this is just

the initial assessment, as you know. It looks to me like she had her throat sliced open with a blade of some sort. Something with a ragged edge. There's also a knife wound at her carotid. Then her eyes were removed with a smaller blade, something with a smooth edge. This was done post-mortem. Not a lot of blood round the wound area.'

'Any sign of the eyes?' Izzie said.

Pamela turned to her. 'Not yet, but they could be anywhere.'

'He took them with him,' Bracken said.

The three of them looked at him.

'I've seen it before. I mean, that's my guess. They could be sitting on the mantelpiece in the old farmhouse for all I know.' Bracken looked at Sullivan. 'Where's the estate agent?'

'He's showing another one of my – your – sergeants around. Checking other buildings with some uniforms and a big dog.'

'I'll want a chat with him.'

'I'll find out where they are.' Sullivan walked away out of the cowshed.

'Thanks, Doc,' Bracken said. 'Nice meeting you.'

'Call me Pam, Sean. I hate being referred to as *Doc*. Makes me feel like I'm in a Bugs Bunny cartoon.'

'Whatever you say.'

'Nice meeting you. I'll be seeing a lot of you,' she said, smiling again. 'And Chaz will too, no doubt.'

The young woman smiled at him and gave a small wave. 'See you around.'

He tried to think on his feet, part terms on a quick shot of wit, but Pam turned away from him and the moment was gone.

'Come on, Izzie, let's find that estate agent,' he said, heading back out into the fresh air.

Outside, he saw Sullivan waving over to him. 'They found something in the old farmhouse,' he said. 'A wallet. Could be the killer's.'

They put the shoe covers in a bin and walked over to where Sullivan was waiting. He walked them around the corner and the wind coming off the Pentlands slapped their cheeks until they were rosy.

The house's windows were boarded up, which surprised Bracken and reminded him of some of the council estates he'd worked over in Glenrothes.

Inside, the house smelled stale if not quite mouldy.

'Been on the market for long?' he asked Sullivan as he and Izzie stepped into the living room after him. A couple of uniforms were standing near a man with an overcoat on. Another detective was close by.

'Sir, this is DS Angela Paton.'

'Sir,' she said, curt and to the point.

'Where's this wallet?' Bracken asked.

One of the uniforms was holding it and he handed it over to Bracken. He took it out of the evidence bag after slipping on some nitrile gloves and opened it up. Inside was a driving licence with a name on it: *Edward Curtis*. He handed it to Sullivan, who had put on gloves in anticipation.

'Wester Hailes. I'll have the team prepare to go talk to him.'

'Hang fire there, Jimmy. I want to be there.'

'Now then, sir,' Bracken said, turning his attention to the man in the suit huddling inside his overcoat. He looked to be in his thirties, with fashionable glasses and slicked-back hair. 'Tell me what happened this morning.'

'I came here expecting to meet with a client who said he was very interested in buying these premises. When I turned up, there was a car in the car park. I thought it was his. Then I saw the barn door was open and thought he had maybe started the tour without me. When I went in, that...young girl was lying there.'

'Did you touch her?'

'What? No. I didn't go near her. She had blood on her. She looked dead. I called the police.'

'And what do you know about this wallet?'

'Nothing. I don't know who this Curtis bloke is. It was lying on the floor when the police officers brought me in.'

'You hadn't been in the farmhouse before we arrived?'

'No. Not at all.'

'Okay. I'll need you to go to the station and make a formal statement.'

Bracken watched as the man, looking glad, was taken out of the smelly old house. 'When we get the time of death, get an alibi from him and do a background check,' he told Sullivan. 'I want to see if there's a madman hiding under all that hair gel.'

'I'll have somebody talk to the people in his office.'

'This is a *just in case* scenario. I don't think he could fight his way through wet bog roll, but stranger things and all that.'

'We'll do the whole shebang on his background. You never know who you're standing next to.'

Bracken thought for a moment that Sullivan was getting in a dig about him and Ailsa, but then dismissed it.

'Let's get that team up to Wester Hailes. And bring one of those big fucking dogs.'

FIVE

The flats looked decent enough from the outside, but it was what was on the inside that made the detectives wear the stab-proof vests. A crackhead with a kitchen knife might get lucky before the boots got flying, and nobody wanted to take a chance.

A man got out of an unmarked car and approached Sullivan. 'He's in there, sir. We called the landline and he answered, and we haven't seen him leave.'

'Thanks,' Sullivan said, then turned to Bracken. 'Ready when you are, sir.'

'Right, son, get Fido there up the stairs,' Bracken said to the dog handler. 'You with the key, get in front there with him. The rest of the entry team next. We'll be right behind. Shock and awe, boys. The scumbag is probably still in bed or he's shoving something up his nose or in his arm. Let's go and make his day.'

The key was a twenty-pound battering ram painted red – so nobody lost it, Bracken always assumed.

The dog was snarling and barking as it went upstairs in search of somebody to have a go at, the handler right behind.

'I wouldn't want that thing hanging off my arse,' Bracken said to Sullivan.

'You and me both, boss.'

'I've seen worse,' Izzie said from behind as a sea of uniforms ran into the building.

'Really? Where?' Bracken said. 'A dog-fighting ring?'

'On TV.'

'Doesn't count,' Bracken said, and then he was up and walking into the stairwell. The warning shouts from the neighbours were too late: he heard the door crashing back on its hinges and Rin Tin Tin was inside, looking for lunch.

By the sound of the screams, he'd found it.

When the detectives got inside, Edward Curtis was standing on the back of the settee against the wall, arms spread out like a tightrope walker. The dog was straining at the leash.

'Get that fucking dog away from me,' the young man said. Despite the cool temperature of the flat, he wore no shirt. No needles were hanging from his arm, and from the look of him, the only thing going up his nose would be a Taser if he didn't come off the settee.

'Eddie Curtis?' Bracken said, stepping forward.

'You can't batter my door in like that. I have rights.'

'You have fuck all. Now get off that settee before we have to tip it over and trample all over you.'

'Do I know you?' Curtis snarled. His hair was all over the place, like he didn't tip his barber well.

Bracken nodded to the handler. 'You can take him back to the van now, son. If we need him to come back up, we'll give you a shout.'

The handler nodded and managed to look disappointed his dog wasn't able to latch on to the man's privates and start swinging from them.

'Right, get your arse down here, and if you try to run, there's a ninety-pound piece of meat on four legs who would love to challenge you to a hundred metre sprint.'

'This is not right,' Curtis said, sliding off the back of the settee to a sitting position. 'What the hell do you lot want anyway? Hey! Mind my TV!' he shouted at a uniform.

'We have a search warrant,' Sullivan said, pulling the piece of paper out of an inside pocket, struggling with it for a second as he got it out from under his vest.

'Why? I haven't done anything.'

'Really?' said Bracken. 'We think you murdered

somebody this morning.'

'What? Fuck off,' Curtis said, trying to act brave but letting his eyes tell the truth.

'Finish getting dressed. We want to have a word with you down at the station.'

'What if I don't want to go?'

'I'll arrest you on suspicion of murder.'

'Christ, what happened to community policing?'

'I never got the memo. Get dressed.'

———

His hair not much improved by a brush, Edward Curtis sat across the table from Bracken and Sullivan in Interview Room 3 at the West End police station, home of MIT West.

His solicitor sat next to him, a pen and paper in front of him. He was a young man who looked like he had drawn the short straw and didn't wear his Legal Aid badge with pride.

'Why don't you start by telling us where you were last night, Edward?' Bracken said.

'I was at home. All night. One of my friends came round. Lisa. She'll verify I was there.'

'Lisa who?' Sullivan asked.

'Aye. She's Chinese.' Curtis grinned.

'I'm glad you think this is funny,' Bracken said.

Racist wee bastard.

'Look, I didn't know that lassie. Why would I want to hurt her?'

'You tell us. Maybe you tried it on with her, things got out of hand and you killed her. It happens.'

'My client said he wasn't with her last night and he's provided an alibi.'

Both detectives looked at the solicitor. He wasn't a high-flyer in his circle of friends and this was bog standard stuff for him.

'An alibi of sorts,' Bracken reminded him. 'We still have to follow up on the alibi witness.'

'How did your wallet get in the farmhouse where she was killed?' Sullivan said.

Curtis shrugged. 'It was stolen.'

Bracken looked at him, not appreciating the games. 'Where was it stolen?'

'I don't know, I swear. I drive a bloke around to all sorts of houses. He's the photographer for an agency that puts schedules together for solicitors who sell houses. I just drive the bloke around and then hang about while he does his thing with the camera.'

'You think he stole your wallet?'

'Ian? Naw. He makes a ton of cash for what he does. Me and him get on like a house on fire. He wouldn't steal my wallet. He's not short of a bob or two, and he drives a nice motor. Well, when he's not half-pished. That's why he employs me as his driver; he's hungover every day.'

'Ian got a last name?'

'Peffers.'

'You didn't have words with him?' Sullivan said. 'Something that would make him take your wallet just to spite you?'

'Not at all.'

'Where do you think you lost your wallet?' Sullivan emphasised the word *lost*.

'We were in the New Town that day. Scotland Street, Henderson Row, Cumberland Street. Another couple. We were really busy, and it wasn't until I went to the boozer that night that I realised it was gone. The next day, we went back and checked the houses, but no sign.'

'And now we've found it in a crappy old farmhouse where there's a dead body, and you want us to believe that you weren't there?' Bracken looked at the man, his eyes drawn to a tuft of hair sticking out at an angle by his left temple. His gut was telling him that this man was telling them the truth. Somehow Bracken couldn't see him killing a woman in the vicious way Andrea Harrison had died.

'Did you drive out to a farm on the outskirts of the city to take photos?'

'No. I've never been to a farm,' Curtis said.

'What about your friend? This Ian?'

'I wouldn't know. I drive him around, and any time I've driven him, he hasn't been to a farm. That's not to say he didn't get an Uber out there, though.'

'We need his full name and contact details,' Sullivan said.

Curtis rattled them off.

'And your female friend's too.'

Once again, Curtis complied.

'Is my client free to go?' the solicitor said, looking at a watch that appeared expensive, though Bracken was leaning towards believing it was a knock-off.

'Don't leave town, Eddie.'

'Like I have the money to do that,' Curtis said, standing up next to the cheap suit. They both left.

'Have somebody check those alibis. Then show me where the coffee is,' Bracken said.

'Will do, sir.'

They both stood up from the table.

'I know you don't officially start until Monday, sir,' said Sullivan, 'and this was supposed to be a day where you familiarised yourself with us and the station, but I thought you would want in on the ground floor on this one.'

'You did good, son. Now show me the coffee before I have to manually peel my tongue off the roof of my mouth.'

SIX

It had been a little over six years since Bracken had set foot in the West End station, but the place looked like it was stuck in some time warp. The smells were the same, and so was the paint job by the look of it.

The management facilities were on the top floor of the old building. It was bereft of any modern convenience such as a lift, and he paused in the ground-floor corridor for a moment. He'd started getting rid of some of his stuff for the move back to Edinburgh, moving most of it into storage. Including his treadmill. He had promised himself he would take up walking while the machine was languishing. Jogging was out of the question; this wasn't Miami after all, and with snow and ice on the ground, if he wasn't quite at the age where breaking a hip could be deadly, then he was certainly knocking on the door.

Now he told himself that running up four flights of stairs constituted a start to his exercise regime. When he got there, he thought he could see a light and hear his old gran calling his name, but after the shooting stars had left his field of vision, he got his breathing under control and walked along a corridor with thoughts of a gym membership at the forefront of his mind. Four flights of stairs and he was fucked. He knew he had to do something about his condition, or else the Grim Reaper would be packing his case and heading his way in no time.

He stopped outside the door he was looking for and knocked.

'Come!'

He opened the door and walked into Detective Superintendent William Burton's office.

'Sean! Come on in. Take a pew.'

'Thank you, sir.' Bracken closed the door and sat down opposite his boss.

'Listen to you; *sir* indeed. How long have we known each other now?'

'Since Adam was a boy.'

'Correct.' Burton laughed. 'I couldn't believe it when I saw your request to transfer back a couple of months ago. I knew you couldn't stay over in the Kingdom for long.'

'Six years is a fair bit of time.'

Burton looked up from his desk and across at Bracken. 'In the grand scheme of things, it's just a wee game of fitba before tea.'

Bracken smiled at his friend and noticed the man had lost weight since he had last seen him. Right about the time of his grandsons' funerals.

'It's good to see you back, Sean,' Burton said again, fiddling with the pencils on his desk. He bent closer to look at them, tutted and sat back up again. 'Bloody cleaner's been touching my pencils again. Christ, why can't she dust round them?'

'It's good to be back.'

'For fuck's sake, that end one just won't stay in place. And where's my wee rubber? God Almighty.'

Bracken leaned forward and moved the rubber eraser from behind a mug. He pushed it across like a chess piece.

'Thanks. That would've driven me bloody daft all day. I think I might have what my wife calls that AC/DC thing.'

'OCD,' Bracken corrected.

'Aye, that. What's it stand for again?'

'Obnoxious, Conceited Dick.'

Burton sat back in his chair and laughed. 'Ya bastard. I missed your wit, Sean, I have to say. Remember the laughs we used to have before you left? Some nights we had in the police club, let me tell you. All I ever remembered was doing a commando crawl to my bed. Many's the night my wife draped a duvet over me.'

'And you blamed me every time for getting you pished.'

Burton laughed again. 'Of course I did.' He leaned forward again and gently nudged a photo frame of his wife and son. 'In the name of Christ. I swear the cleaner does this on purpose.'

'She does it to annoy you, and I can see it's working.'

'You heard about my Tommy?' The question caught Bracken off-guard for a moment, but he nodded.

'I did, Billy. It was a shock to us all.'

Burton stopped playing with his things and looked across at his DCI. 'I tried talking to him, but nothing would bring him out of it. Depression's a bastard, Sean. It took my wee boy. He had nothing to live for, he said, with his wife and boys gone.'

'It was tragic.'

'I was the one who found him. Thank God he took an overdose and didn't step in front of a train.'

Bracken didn't know if the man was being serious or flippant.

'You went to the crime scene with Sullivan,'

Burton said, as if the thought of his dead son had simply vanished out of his head.

'He called to ask me to meet him there, yes.'

'Bastard, eh? You were supposed to start on Monday, but here we are, the day before the weekend, and somebody throws this in your lap. Welcome to Edinburgh.' Burton wasn't smiling anymore, and it seemed that all his little knickknacks were in their own spots again. 'Sullivan told me about the eyes.'

Bracken nodded. 'They haven't found them yet.'

'And they won't.' Burton pointing a finger at him. 'Whoever did this is copying that fucking bitch. We know she's still in the Royal Edinburgh. Hell, I was even invited to her wedding. But now somebody has decided to kill a lassie and do the same to her as Ailsa Connolly did to her victims.'

Bracken was about to ask why Burton had got an invite and he hadn't, but it would have sounded weird. He was still smarting over the lack of a phone call.

'Who's her husband?' he asked instead.

'Dr Robert Marshall. Another psychologist. He knew her way back and started writing to her in the hospital, and she wrote back and the rest is history.'

'We should talk to him.'

'I'll leave that with you, Sean. You have a good team here, so use them as needed.'

'I will, Billy. Sullivan looks like a good guy. Izzie seems competent too.'

'You met Charlie Nelson?'

'I have.'

Burton shook his head. 'Laddie goes about like he's on fucking glue. He's sailing close to the wind. Keep him in line.'

One more fiddle with a pencil and Burton stood up and held his hand out. 'Glad you're back with us, my friend.'

Bracken stood up. 'Good to be back. Now we just need to see about getting a lift installed.'

'Or you could buy an exercise bike like I did,' Burton replied. 'It's also good for hanging shirts on.'

SEVEN

Down to the next level and the team were busy in the incident room. Jimmy Sullivan turned when he saw Bracken enter.

'You find Superintendent Burton's office alright?' he asked.

'Aye. I've been here before of course, but I was based in Gayfield Square.' *Not so many stairs in there,* he was about to add, but he was sure they could see the sweat on his brow for themselves without his adding any finishing touches to their impression of him.

'Izzie has the whiteboard going,' Sullivan pointed out.

Bracken looked around the room, like a schoolboy coming into a high school class for the first time, the new boy in an already established class. It was an old room, the ghosts of detectives past still lingering in the woodwork. The only nod to modern policing was the computers on the desks. He'd had reason to come here once many years ago when he was starting out and an established DCI had chewed him out for walking in and interrupting a powwow between the men. There hadn't been women on this man's team – whether by design or coincidence, Bracken wasn't quite sure. He wondered how long the old guy had been gone. His attitude wouldn't have been tolerated in this day and age.

'Your office is over on the left,' Sullivan said.

Bracken looked at the door leading into the room. Blinds had been pulled down, affording some privacy, and the room brought back memories of the rollicking he'd had.

'That's fine. I'll put my coat in there later.' He shrugged out of it and hung it on the back of a chair.

DC Charlie Nelson turned round from a table in the corner. 'Tea or coffee, sir?'

'What?' Bracken said.

'What's your poison?'

'Oh. Coffee. Milk, no sugar.'

'We only use powdered milk on account of us drinking some that wasn't quite of the fresh variety and some of us had the sh–'

'Powdered is fine,' Bracken said, holding up a hand.

'I said I was sorry,' said a young woman at a desk.

'Sir, this is DS Angela Paton. Angie, this is our new boss, DCI Bracken.'

The woman stood up and smiled at him. She looked to be in her early thirties; blonde hair with dark hair tucked behind the blonde.

'Pleased to meet you, sir.'

'You too.'

'DCI Bracken, for those of you who've forgotten, ran an MIT in Glenrothes but has transferred back to Edinburgh,' Sullivan said.

Nelson came over with the coffee and held it out for the boss to take.

'You washed your hands, I see,' Bracken said, grabbing hold of it.

'I'm sorry?' Nelson said. Then, 'Oh, aye. The cow shite. They say it's good for the skin, so I heard.'

'Not for mine it isn't, and count yourself lucky you didn't manage to get any of it on me.'

'Where did you hear it was good for your skin?' Izzie asked.

Nelson shrugged. 'I don't know. I just read it somewhere.'

'In the back of one of your filthy mags, no doubt.'

'She means my car mags,' Nelson explained to Bracken.

Sailing close to the wind, Burton had said about Nelson, and Bracken knew what he meant now.

'I'd like to summarise what we have already from this morning's case,' Bracken said, putting the mug down on a desk. He sat on the chair and looked at the whiteboard.

'I brought them up to speed on the interview with Eddie Curtis,' Sullivan said.

'Are we sure he's not on the hook for this?' Angie said.

'You know the old saying: the show's not over –'

'Till Angie sings,' Nelson said, grinning into his mug of coffee.

'Piss off, Charlie.'

Bracken looked at them, which was enough to stop the comedy duo going further.

'Of course we haven't fully ruled out Curtis yet,' he said. 'His wallet was at the scene of the crime, but all that means is, his wallet was there. Doesn't mean *he* was there. He said his wallet was stolen. It could also mean he *was* there and he dropped the wallet after killing Andrea Harrison. Did anybody do a check?'

'I did,' Izzie said. 'His bank received a phone call about his bank card being missing a week ago. It was cancelled and a new one was issued. Same with his other cards, a couple of credit cards with low limits.'

'Did you get to talk to the man he drives about? Ian Peffers?'

'Yes, we spoke to him. He confirmed Curtis's story

about losing the wallet and them going back to some properties to look for it and not finding it.'

'Could still be an elaborate smokescreen,' Bracken said. 'Did you run a check on the other cards in his wallet?'

'We did. They were cards that were reported lost. We can't find any connection yet.'

'We're still trying to trace the female he said he was with last night. If she confirms his alibi, then he'll be put on the back burner,' Sullivan said.

Bracken loosened his tie a little. The old radiators were playing a tune as they pumped out the heat.

'I want the names of any people who had shown interest in buying that farm, or at least in going to look at it, and make sure that estate agent's alibi is checked out. Although by the look of him, he wouldn't want to have a hair out of place, far less get into a tussle with a lassie and kill her. Also, check out who currently owns the farm. Somebody chose that spot to kill Andrea.'

'Yes, sir,' Angie said.

'What about next of kin?' Bracken asked.

'We've contacted Andrea's office and they've furnished us with details,' Sullivan said.

'Did you find out if she lives alone?'

'Lives with her parents.'

'Right, while we're having Curtis's alibi checked

out, I want you and me to go and talk to the next of kin, Jimmy,' Bracken said.

'I'll get my jacket.'

'Meantime, liaise with forensics,' he said to Angie. 'See if they've come up with anything. I doubt it, considering the location, but you never know. I'll call the pathologist later.'

'Will do, sir.'

They watched as Bracken pulled his overcoat back on and left the incident room with Sullivan.

EIGHT

'Fife?' Bracken said again as Sullivan settled himself behind the wheel. 'Why in God's name does Andrea Harrison's name sound so familiar?'

'Rhetorical?'

'Thinking out loud. I know that name from somewhere, but maybe I'm getting my wires crossed from somewhere else. Maybe a friend of my daughter's or something.'

Sullivan drove through Haymarket, joining the line of rush hour traffic as darkness descended.

The chaos and madness was only going to get worse.

'You just got the one?' Sullivan asked.

'One what?' Bracken looked at him as if he had just had the piss taken out of him and hadn't realised it.

'Kid. You mentioned your daughter a minute ago.'

'Oh, yeah. She's twenty-one and at uni. Didn't want to go away to study, but she still wanted to experience college life. She stays in a flat with some yahoos.'

The exhaust fumes from the cars spewed into the cold evening air, swirling around in the sea of red taillights.

'What about you?' Bracken asked the younger DI.

'Two. Boy and a girl. Ten and seven. Real handful, but I wouldn't be without them.' Sullivan sprayed windscreen wash, the wipers grinding over the filthy glass.

'Enjoy them while they're young, son. Before you know it, they'll be grown up and have wee yins of their own.'

'You a grandpa yet?'

'No. If some bastard touches my wee lassie, he'll be fucking marrying her.'

The traffic flowed across the new bridge that spanned the Forth and Sullivan took the turn for Dunfermline. Bracken heard his stomach growl even though dinnertime was a way off.

He took out his phone and called Mary at the guest house. Told her not to be keeping any dinner for him, that he would pick something up from the chippie. Sullivan could hear the raised voice on the other end.

When he hung up, Bracken said, 'I'm staying at a guest house that belongs to a former DI, Bob –'

'Long,' Sullivan interrupted. 'I heard. He pops into the station now and again.'

'His wife treats me like a long-lost son. She's a really special lady.'

'Bob likes to think so,' Sullivan said, looking at the maps on his phone, which was stuck on a holder that poked out of the air vents.

'Christ, I remember getting ready to go to the police club on a Friday night,' Bracken said. 'Getting ready for a sesh with Billy Burton and the rest of the crew. We had some fine times there. Now look at me: sitting in a car with Niki fucking Lauda, going to some old dearie's place to tell her that her daughter's been murdered. Christ, I could never get used to this bit. Especially if they start crying.'

'It's just her dad. Mum passed away a couple of years ago.'

'It's worse when the dad starts crying,' Bracken replied as Sullivan pulled the car over at the side of the road.

Snow was started to fall from a sky that was dark but not quite pitch black. The house was large and detached and would have fetched twice as much if it were in Edinburgh rather than Dunfermline. Still, the golf course was only a three iron away.

The houses were cookie cutter, with only three different designs that Bracken could make out, but it was a nice neighbourhood, the sort of place you wouldn't expect to come home to find your neighbour tanning your house.

Sullivan turned the engine off and they looked into the house from the warmth of the car, neither of them making a move. They saw a man come into the living room and sit down in front of a TV. The blinds were still open, as if he hadn't realised darkness was coming.

Bracken was the first to open the door and step out into the cold falling snow. Footsteps from strangers littered the pavement, compacting the snow into the shape of shoes and boots.

'You play golf, sir?' Sullivan asked.

'Not knocking the game, son, but I could find better ways to spend an afternoon.'

'I don't think it's too bad – bit of exercise walking about, having a laugh with your pals, few sociable beers. I could think of worse hobbies.'

'Championship flower arranging.'

Sullivan had to admit that flowers weren't his thing. 'Except when I've pissed off my wife. Then they always come in handy.'

'Many's the time when a bunch from a petrol station mended some fences. How about you? Play golf?'

'Oh, I wish. Every spare moment is spent playing with my kids. Sometimes I would kill to play golf.'

Bracken looked at him for a moment. The DI's face was lit by the automatic light that illuminated their approach.

'You know what I mean,' Sullivan said.

'You and I haven't worked together before, but I'm assuming that you've been on one of these jaunts before, so just don't open your mouth and jump in with both feet.'

'Never have done, sir, and don't intend to start now.'

'Glad to hear it.' Bracken put a gloved finger against the doorbell.

'Mr Harrison?' he said when the older man opened the door.

'Yes?'

Bracken held up his warrant card and introduced himself and his DI.

'What's wrong? Is it Andrea?'

'We need to step inside, sir.'

The man stood to one side and almost sucked his gut in to let them pass.

'First on the right,' Harrison said, closing the door behind them. Which was the living room they'd seen him sitting in just a few minutes ago. It was clean and well looked after and Bracken wondered if Harrison had always kept the house this spick and span, or whether the death of his wife had kicked it into gear.

Harrison came in behind them and grabbed the remote, silencing the TV, if not quite making the picture disappear. A meal sat on a tray table, something that had been popped into the microwave. One-nil for the cleaning versus cooking.

'Is it about Andrea?' he asked again.

Bracken could feel his face starting to go red, the heat in the house keeping the cold at bay. He loosened his tie a fraction.

'It is. We found a body this morning and we believe it to be your daughter, Andrea.'

'Oh fuck,' Harrison said, and more fell than sat back in the chair. 'My wee girl, dead?' He looked at the detectives like he had misheard Bracken, and when he realised a mistake had been made, they could all have a laugh about it and go on their merry way.

But Bracken hadn't made a mistake. Harrison could see that.

'I'm so sorry, Mr Harrison, but we need to ask you some questions. We believe Andrea was murdered.'

Bracken nodded for Sullivan to take a seat, then he sat on the couch near the grieving father, whose head was now lowered while his shoulders bobbed up and down. Bracken gave him a moment before talking again.

'This is not going to be easy, but we really do need to ask. Did Andrea have a partner?'

Harrison looked up at him, tears now running down his cheeks. 'Nobody special.' He ran a sleeve across his eyes and Bracken felt sorry for the man. The room had a china cabinet in one corner with little ornaments inside, and Bracken wondered if the man was keeping a clean house in case somebody had made a mistake and his wife was coming back one day.

'A boyfriend? Husband?' Sullivan asked.

'I told her that bastard was no good,' Harrison said, the tears held back for a moment so he could get the anger out.

'Who is this?' Bracken asked.

'Some bloke she was seeing on the side. I mean, he was the one who was messing her about. He's married. We were arguing and she blurted out that he had a wife and kids. I told her not to get involved, but she told me she was having fun and I could go fuck myself. Christ, it was the last time I spoke to her.'

'When was this?'

'Night before last. She was going out straight from work last night. I wish I had made more of an effort. But no, I lectured her.' Then Harrison sat up straighter as if he had just thought of something. 'I'll kill the bastard if he did something to her.'

'Did she give you his name?' Bracken asked.

'Peter. Although that was probably a fake name if he was married. There are a lot of bastards out there who will lead women on just to get their way with them, then sneak back to the wife. This joker was obviously one of them. I'll wring his fucking neck.'

'We don't want to jump to conclusions,' Sullivan said. 'This is the start of the investigation and we want to apprehend the person who did this.'

'I know. But I don't know of one single person who didn't like my Andrea.'

'Do you know where she met him?' Sullivan asked.

'She just said she bumped into him, literally, in some pub. They were having their Christmas piss-up. This was a couple of weeks ago, when offices start going to these do's early. They hit it off and she started seeing him.'

'And you don't know exactly where they met?' Sullivan said.

'Somewhere in the city centre. That's all she would tell me.'

'Where did she work?' Bracken asked.

'She was a paralegal for McHenry, Branston and Harvey. Solicitors in Edinburgh.'

And then it hit Bracken. Now he knew where he'd heard the name Andrea Harrison before.

She'd worked on the Ailsa Connolly case.

NINE

Bracken could hear chatter from the dining room in the guest house when he got in. He stamped his feet to get the snow off his boots, then took his overcoat off. He was about to go upstairs when Mary came into the hallway.

'There's still dinner, Sean. Plenty to go around.'

'I was going to go to the chippie. I don't want you to go to any trouble.'

'Och, away with yourself. Hang your coat up there and come through and meet the other guests. Chippie indeed, Sean Bracken. Good home cooking is what you need.'

'I can't argue with that, Mary.'

'How have you managed all these years without Catherine cooking for you?' she said, leading the way down the hall.

Bracken hesitated for a second. 'Chippie,' he said, remembering how fucked he'd felt earlier running up the stairs in the station. 'Aye, maybe it's time for a wee change.'

'I'll say it is,' she replied, leading him into the guests' dining room. The faces at the small tables looked at him. 'Everybody, this is our new guest, Sean Bracken. He's a detective, like Bob was.'

'Nobody move. This is a raid and you're all under arrest,' Bracken said.

Nobody moved or said a word; they merely stared at him.

'Tough audience,' he said to Mary. Then to the others, 'I'm just kidding.'

An old woman laughed. 'I knew you were, son. Sit yourself down.'

'I didn't know,' said the old man sitting at her table. 'I think I peed myself.'

'Stop exaggerating, old fool.'

'This is Mr and Mrs Clark, the couple I told you about,' Mary said.

'Only good things, I hope?' Mr Clark said.

'I just want to say, I didn't believe a word of what Mary said,' Bracken told him. Mrs Clark laughed. Mr Clark looked like he was trying to remember what drawer he'd put his stash of weed in.

'And this young lady is my niece, Natalie Hogan.' Mary beamed at the young woman.

'Pleased to meet you, Mr Bracken,' Natalie said.

'Likewise.'

'We thought we were going to be busier this time of year, but we're not. Nice and cosy, though,' said Mary. 'But sit yourself down and I'll get your dinner. As you can see, the others are already onto dessert. Apple pie and ice cream.'

The diet of fat bastards everywhere, myself included, Bracken thought. But it would be rude to refuse a good piece of apple pie.

Bracken sat at a table next to Natalie. She looked to be in her thirties, with blonde hair pulled back into a ponytail. She wore jeans and a lumberjack shirt.

'You staying here long?' she asked him.

'Just until I can get my own place sorted. I worked with Bob a while back. What about you?'

'I live here. On my own. Nowhere else to go.' She spooned the rest of the pie into her mouth. Bracken was impressed that she was so slim but still managed to get some pie down her. He would ask what her secret was later on. Unless she had a home gym in her room. Or stuck her fingers down her throat.

'Will you be here for Christmas?' Mr Clark asked, and it was evident in his face that he knew there was more chance of seeing Santa than Bracken not being here.

'Looks like I will be, yes.'

'Oh, that's good,' the old man replied with all the enthusiasm of a guy who'd just learned that he had six weeks to live and the man in the next bed didn't wear the same size slippers.

'I'm sure we'll all enjoy each other's company,' Mary said. 'Bob will have too much to drink and start singing before having to be put to bed.'

'Nothing wrong with my vocal cords,' Bob said, coming into the room.

'If we were tone deaf.' She smiled at him, giving a little laugh.

'Oh, I don't know, a little bit of cabaret after Christmas dinner sounds just the ticket,' Bracken said.

'Don't you start,' Bob said, shaking his head. 'That's all I need, people ganging up on me...'

TEN

Back then

Dr Robert Marshall walked into the pub and wondered if he should just skip the bar and go straight to the bathroom where he could slit his wrists.

'A wee dram, Bob?' his friend Tam asked from the end of the bar. 'You look like you need it.'

'Aye, that would be a grand idea, my friend.'

Two drams in hand, they found a little table along from the open fire where logs were spitting out sparks.

'Cheers,' Robert said.

'Why the long face? Another deviant?'

'This job gets worse and worse. I became a doctor to help people, but this having to talk to mutants who are only in my office because of a court order gets right under my skin. They don't pay me enough, Tam.'

'If you want to talk about it, I'm all ears, you know that.'

'I know, chum.'

Robert never talked about his work with anybody. Doing so would go against everything he stood for.

Tam was different. They went back a long way, back to a darker time when Tam's son was dealing with some troubles. Not knowing where to turn, his son decided the only way out was to take his own life. Robert talked him out of it that night, and sat with him for many hours afterwards, always there for him when he felt himself slipping down the slope. Not once did Robert ever think it was an imposition; he just stepped forward each and every time.

That was why Tam was always there for Robert when he needed a shoulder.

'If you want to talk –'

'He sodomised the girl.' Robert finished his whisky, stood up and went to the bar. Soon enough, two pints and another two nips sat on the table. Robert drank some of the real ale before he continued.

'The wee bastard admitted to me that he sodomised the lassie before he stabbed her and left her for dead. That was never revealed in court, Tam, but the little fucker revealed it to me. And you know what?'

Tam shook his head, indicating that he did indeed not know what. Robert took a swig of his ale and made sure he kept his voice down and nobody was eaves-dropping.

'He smiled when he said it. Looked me in the fucking eye and smiled, nodding his head like he was proud of it. Can you believe that? He told me he knew exactly what he was doing. And that he enjoyed it more than anything.'

'That's fucked-up. Can't you report him?' Tam had a disgusted look on his face.

'I can't. He could be making it up. He has a low IQ. It's my job to keep him on the straight and narrow, and he'll work towards trying to convince me that he's better now, that he's cured. But he'll go right back to doing what he likes doing. It's been four years since the attack and I think he's prepping for something bigger. I'll write that in my report of course, but I think he'll reoffend and there's not a damn thing anybody will do about it.'

'That's fucking sick. I hope some bastard sticks it to him one day.'

'Me too, Tam. I don't think I can do this job much longer.'

Ailsa Connolly made sure Robert Marshall had an alibi before making her move. She watched him walk into the pub and meet his friend before driving off.

Ricky Daniels was easy to find. He hung around the shopping centre long after most of the shops had shut, their metal shutters keeping out the likes of him.

The little corner store was the last to close. Daniels always seemed to find somebody to buy him a bottle of booze. He drank on his own this night, in the dark shadows of a closed shop. Maybe looking for new prey, maybe just enjoying the good old Scottish pastime of underage drinking.

Whatever, Ailsa found him sitting alone. Of course, the idea wasn't to engage him, but to get close enough, just like somebody might get close enough to a lion at the zoo, knowing there was glass between the animal and them. There was no glass between Ailsa and Daniels, but she had to get close enough to arouse his attention.

No decent person was here after dark. It was strictly a playground for the wicked.

She wore tracksuit trousers and a hoody pulled up. Black, just like the night. She looked at him briefly, making eye contact, then hurried on towards the underpass that went beneath the dual carriageway.

She heard the glass bottle being put on the pavement and knew then that he was following her. She didn't want to look back and alert him. If he grabbed her from behind, that would mean more work for her, but the end result would be the same.

The underpass was poorly lit and smelled of piss. Ailsa didn't hear anything but was listening intently. Then it came: the shuffle of a shoe catching the concrete.

Then the slap of running feet very close to her. No shouts, no nothing – the lion moving in for the kill. She tensed. Timing had to be right. She turned fast and brought the leather sap out and hit him on the temple with it, not hard enough to kill him, but sufficient to make his legs go weak.

Then she put his arm around her shoulders and half-carried him to her car. Anybody who might have seen them would see two drunk people. And in this neighbourhood, it was more suspicious if you looked like you were sober.

The room was damp and dark and smelled like something had died in it recently. Which it had.

Ricky Daniels sniffed the air, trying not to take a

deep breath. What the fuck was this place? Water dripped in another room. He could barely see, the room made up of shadows and half-seen objects.

The chair he was sitting on was hard, like the old, shitty ones his mother had in their house. Was that where he was? Maybe he'd fallen and had gone blind and somehow he was an invalid now, like his old fart of a grandpa. He was an invalid and didn't think twice about reminding people at every opportunity, quickly followed by telling anybody who would listen how old he was and how marvellous he was for his age.

'Hello, Ricky,' said a faint voice, like a whisper.

'Mum?' Daniels said, moving his eyes, but still he couldn't see properly.

Then a light came on, but it just made the shadows brighter. Until the hood was whipped off his head. He squinted against the brightness of the light, which was shining right into his eyes. He tried putting a hand up to shield his eyes from the light but couldn't. Then the light was moved over to one side.

The room was old and decrepit. He saw that the chair was on a carpet. A settee was opposite him, with a little table at the side. Almost like it was a living room from a nightmare.

The woman, definitely not his mum, sat on the couch looking at him.

'Who are you?' he asked her, not an ounce of fear in his voice or expression. Anger sat inside him like a smouldering fire. A woman tying him up? What the fuck?

'My name is not important. If that's what you're asking. In another context, I am the woman who wants to talk to you.'

He looked into her eyes and it slowly came back to him. The bitch from the underpass.

'Untie me.'

'Like you untied Maisie? You didn't tie her, though, did you, Ricky?' Ailsa Connolly smiled at him. 'You do remember what happened, even though it's been a few years. When you were just a boy. A twelve-year-old boy who your solicitor said had a mental capacity of under eight years old, the legal age of responsibility. And it worked. You went into psychiatric care and spent five months of a two-year sentence in custody until they released you. Then you attacked another girl two years ago, but there was insufficient evidence and you walked free. Then a few weeks ago, same thing. Now you're eighteen and an adult.'

'What are you fucking talking about? Get me off this chair or I'll –'

'Or you'll do what?' Ailsa said, interrupting him.

'Untie me and I'll show you what I did to that

bitch. I'll have tears running down your cheeks, just like she had.' He started thrashing about on the chair, to no avail.

'We're here tonight to talk about your punishment, Ricky.' Ailsa smiled at him.

Daniels stopped rocking the chair. 'I've already been punished.' He laughed. 'That's a fucking joke, the whole justice system. Old ponces in funny wigs arguing about my sanity and how I was only a wee boy. I played the system and they took it all in. Just like that silly bitch I touched.'

'That's right, the one you sodomised and left scarred for the rest of her life.'

'She was asking for it!' Daniels was snarling now.

'She was sixteen, at a party with her friends.' Ailsa kept her voice even, not letting any emotion creep in. Even showing anger to him would let him win.

'Her dress was barely a dress. She was flirting. Asking for it. So I gave her it.'

Silence now, just the sounds of the night outside – not many, considering their location.

'That's all water under the bridge now, Ricky. As I said, we're here to discuss your punishment.'

'You related to her, the girl I touched? Is that it? You want revenge for her? Why don't you untie me and you can have a go?'

'Oh, I'm not going to fight you, but you saw in the underpass that you will never be a match for me. You saw how easy it was for me to overpower you and administer a little something so we could drive over here.'

There was uncertainty on his face now, like things had just got real.

'Okay, I'm sorry, okay? There, I've said it. Just let me go.'

Ailsa stood up and slowly walked over to him. She stood and looked at him for a second. Then she stepped out of view for a moment and he heard rustling, and when she came back into view, she was wearing a paper suit like the ones worn at a crime scene. The hood was pulled over her head and only her face was showing, but she flipped down a visor.

'Not going to lie to you, this is going to hurt a lot. You'll die of course, but before that, I'm going to give you a little taste of your own medicine.'

For the first time in his life, Ricky Daniels felt real fear. Just before the blade sliced into him.

It took him two hours to die, and he wasn't seen again. There was a small article about a young thug going missing, but the news soon faded.

He wouldn't be found until five years later, a year after Ailsa's incarceration, when she would bring people back to the farm so they could dig him up. He was Ailsa's first victim but would be listed as victim number six.

He was the catalyst for everything that happened next.

When she was finished, Ailsa casually got back into her car and drove home, smiling all the way.

ELEVEN

'I have to admit, I do like a wee dram now and again,' Bob Long said as he and Bracken settled back into chairs in the residents' lounge. 'Mary tells me to drink in our own lounge, but where's the fun in that? There's usually somebody kicking about. Mr Clark sometimes joins me and we talk about his old war days and I bore him to death with my police stories. Then we both end up blootered. Round off the night with a few Frank Sinatra numbers.'

'You're not old enough to appreciate Ol' Blue Eyes.'

'That's what Spotify's for, son.'

'Here's to Frank.'

They clinked glasses and Bracken took a swig of beer from his bottle and put it back on the little side table.

'Mr Clark not coming down tonight?' Bracken asked, feeling the heat from the electric fire seep into him. By Christ, he would be knocking that down to two bars in a little while, but for now it felt good.

'It takes him a little while to warm to people. He doesn't trust strangers, not after what happened.'

'What happened?' Bracken said after Bob left the invitation open for him to ask.

'His bastard son cleaned them both out. House, savings, the fucking lot.'

'How did he manage that?'

Bob shook his head and knocked back the whisky before topping their glasses up. 'They gave him power of attorney. He sold their house right from underneath them. They went on a three-week holiday to Spain and when they came back, they found somebody else moving into their house. The little bastard had kept the price low to attract buyers, and they came crawling.'

'Jesus, that's rough.'

'Know what I would have done? Taken a bulldozer to the house. But that's just me.'

'And he stole their money too?'

'Ah! See, technically it wasn't stealing. He had his name on their accounts. He just waltzed in and started making withdrawals. Left something like fifty quid in the accounts. Mrs Clark had to be taken to the Royal. Poor old bugger collapsed.'

'And where is this son now?' asked Bracken.

'They haven't seen him in six months. The last they heard, he was shacking up with some fucking crack whore in Dunfermline.'

'What's his name?'

'Roddy Clark. Why?'

'Nothing. I could call some of my old colleagues, see if they've heard of him.'

'He hasn't broken any laws, Sean. That's the worst thing about it.'

'How long have the Clarks been here?'

'They came just after the summer season died down. They were living in sheltered accommodation, but a niece in Australia wired them some money to keep them ticking over. Mr Clark came to me and Mary and asked if he could rent a room for a month. We got talking one night and he said he was trying to find somewhere else. Said he and Mrs Clark had new bank accounts and he had a pension coming in, and the social work department were helping them find a place to live. We cut them some slack and they live here now. We take just enough to cover expenses and don't make a profit from them.'

'I hope you're not thinking you're not going to be making a profit off me, Bob. I'll pay the going rate.'

'Och, away you go, man.'

'Bollocks. You and Mary are running a business.'

'If I can't help out the man who saved my life, then who the hell can I help?' Bob took another sip of whisky, his lip trembling.

'I told you we were even a long time ago, Bob.'

'Aye, well, we didn't see anybody else running into that burning building to get me out. You were there first, in front of those firefighters. Me and those two kids, all dragged out by somebody I thought was an apparition, but it was my best friend. You.' Bob held up his glass and they clinked again.

'You would have done the same thing for me,' Bracken said.

'Yeah, so I would have. Your arse would have been toast.' Bob laughed. 'If only I hadn't broken my back.'

'You thought you were saving two little kids overcome by smoke. You weren't to know they had been murdered.'

They both sat staring at the fire for a moment. Then Bob said to Bracken, 'I hate her, Sean. Hate her with every fibre of my being. I know that's an old cliché, but by God, I hate the fucking bitch.'

'Ailsa Connolly still denies killing those kids.'

Bob's head snapped round fast. 'I know she does. She should own up to what she did. But no, she's still lying about it. You know what I think?'

Bracken shook his head to indicate that no, he

didn't know what Bob thought, but he was about to find out anyway.

'They built that new Royal Edinburgh at the back of the old one. Nice new secure wing. So they could accept Grade A patients. High security. Before, there were only low- and medium-security patients. By building that wing, they could take the pressure off Carstairs. And now Ailsa Connolly lives there in a nice, comfortable wing all by herself. She wouldn't have got the transfer if she'd admitted killing those kiddies.'

'She doesn't have the whole unit to herself, Bob.'

'I know that, but she has her own wee wing because she's the only female there. The other heid-bangers have to share a wing, but that bitch gets a special place to herself.'

'She's still locked-up. She's not going anywhere.'

Bob laughed, but his teeth were bared. 'You not get any newspapers over there, son?'

'What do you mean?'

'I mean, Ailsa Connolly wasn't given a whole-life order like she might have been because she wasn't deemed fit for trial. Diminished responsibility because of the abuse she suffered at the hands of her father. Which means that, in theory at least, she can be set free if a doctor deems her fit to return to society.'

'I know all that. She's never going to get out.'

Bob laughed like somebody might laugh at a young thug who'd just cut him off in his car and was now through a hedge, upside down. 'I beg to differ. This is what she's been aiming for all this time. Fool them into believing that she's not a nut job anymore. Start by getting the transfer to the new Royal Edinburgh. She's been there three years. Two years ago, she started a degree in theology.'

'Theology?'

'Something like that, Sean. She's heading towards a Bachelor's in Divinity, whatever it's called. She's going to be a Church of Scotland minister.'

Bracken looked at his friend like he'd had a stroke. 'Minister? How the hell can she become a minister?'

Again, Bob came out with a strange little laugh, like he was in some sort of trance. 'Haven't you heard, mate? We're in the twenty-first century. People can do what they want nowadays and nobody says a word. Ailsa Connolly wanted to become a minister, and apparently you have to go to some conference thing first, before you can be considered. And what do you know? They let her go to one, under supervision. And she talked her way into the programme.'

Bracken swallowed his whisky and held out his glass for his friend to fill. 'I'm assuming that she's doing it for fun? You know, to prove a point.'

'You know what they say about assuming something: assume makes a right arse out of both of us. But to answer your question, if Ailsa ever gets out, she'll be able to have a mentor for fifteen months, another qualified minister, and then have her own parish. I tell you, mate, I looked into all of this, and you couldn't make it up. Can you imagine her having her own flock? She'd kill them all.'

'It must be hard for her to study in the hospital, surely?' Bracken was sweating now, glad he wasn't wearing his tie.

'Nope. She gets all the time she needs to study. And once a month, she gets to go up to the place on the Mound and hang out with other students. Under supervision.'

'I didn't think they would give her a bus fare, Bob.'

Bob poured himself more whisky. 'Just saying. She could murder a whole fucking class, but nobody's worried.'

'Who sanctioned this?' Bracken asked.

'The justice minister. That new guy who thinks he walks on water. Some left-wing radical who thinks we should be letting half of those crooked bastards out of prison and helping them integrate into society better. Obviously, he's never drunk in Craigmillar on a Saturday night.'

'They're taking a hell of a risk.'

'Not according to the clinical director. He's assured

everybody that Ailsa is getting better. In fact, he reckons she's come on leaps and bounds over the past few years. I just know they're going to release her. Suddenly, she'll be cured and off she'll go. Poor Ailsa Connolly had a breakdown and killed those men, but now her nightmare is over and she can be a respectable member of the community again. Just sleep with one eye open.'

Both men sat in contemplative silence for a few moments before Bracken steered the conversation away to something else.

'I spoke to Billy Burton today. Christ, it's been a long time since I saw him.'

'God, you remember the days we drank in the police club?'

'How could I forget?' Bracken remembered going to the club many times, but sometimes he couldn't remember how he had got to bed. Billy Burton was a drinking machine.

'It was a shame about his laddie.' Bob's voice was quiet. 'I can understand why the poor bastard did it.' He looked at Bracken. 'Took his own life, I mean.'

'Christ, don't be saying that, Bob.'

'Those little boys were dead before I got to them. We didn't know that when we saw the house on fire. Billy Burton's grandchildren. Ailsa Connolly getting back at him. The wee boys and their mother, all dead.

Burton's laddie couldn't cope, couldn't live his life any longer without them. He wanted to join them. That's what the note said, so I heard. Poor bastard.'

'Aye, it must be hard for Billy, knowing his son and grandkids are all dead, and his daughter-in-law.'

'They stopped hanging far too soon in this country, if you ask me.'

'What about his wife?'

'He didn't tell you? She has dementia. Doesn't know what day it is half the time.'

Bracken felt their conversation had turned a corner and was about to start talking about cartoons just to lighten the mood. Maybe the Coyote would get the Road Runner in the next episode. Maybe Yosemite Sam would blow the fucking rabbit to smithereens.

Then the lounge door opened and Bracken smiled when he saw who it was.

'Oh, I'm sorry, I didn't mean to interrupt. I thought the lounge was empty. I'll just go back to my room,' Natalie said.

'What? Oh, don't be daft,' Bracken said. 'Bob won't mind if you join us.' *Please, God.*

'No, you come away in, hen. I think I'll go through to the back house. If you don't mind, Sean. I need to take some painkillers.'

'You go right ahead there, pal. You have a long day without me keeping you up.' Bracken looked briefly at the clock on the mantelpiece; 8.04. 'Bloody party animal.'

Bob laughed and looked like he was struggling to get out of his chair. Bracken was about to get up and give him a hand when Natalie grabbed hold of his arm and pulled.

'Thanks, love. You working tomorrow?'

Natalie shook her head. 'Sunday.'

'Right. If you have a lie-in and don't make it down for breakfast, I'll save some for you.'

She laughed. 'No lie-in for me. Laundry to be done. And other chores.'

'I feel bad that you do that.'

'I offered, remember? Gives me something to do.'

Bob patted her on the arm. 'You're a good lass.' Then he turned to Bracken. 'Remember what I said; it won't be long before we have to start looking over our shoulders.'

TWELVE

'I've told you, my wife's friend saw us together and now she's asking questions. We just have to lie low for a little while longer. It won't be long, I promise.'

He looked in the rear-view mirror, catching a glimpse of himself as the car behind shone its lights right into his. He hoped she wouldn't notice that he'd trimmed a little bit off his hair at the sides with the aid of a pair of scissors and a prayer. More dye had taken care of the colour, the stuff that washed out. He would rinse it all out when he got home, as long as this silly bitch didn't mention anything.

It wouldn't matter if she did. He would just make sure there was no blood in the car.

'I hate all this creeping about. It makes me uneasy.' Maggie Scott smiled at him in the darkness. They were in a country road now, little used and no streetlights.

'It won't be for long, I promise. I'm telling her this week. I just need to move some assets about, so she doesn't get her filthy mitts on them. We don't want to be paupers now, do we?'

She giggled. That was one thing about her; the enthusiasm. So long as he was chucking some dosh about, she was happy.

'Remember we're going to Paris at the end of the month. As long as you haven't told anybody.'

'Oh, I wanted to tell my bestie so much, but I remembered what you said about us not being able to go if your wife found out.'

'That's right. Just another few weeks and you can take out an advert in the local paper if you like.'

'Oh, Peter, I love you so much.'

'I love you too, honey.' *Jesus.* He shivered at the idea of marrying this shallow bitch. Thank God this was all a game. He almost put his fingers into his mouth, feigning making himself sick, but smiled instead.

'I have a surprise for you,' he said, slowing the BMW down. He put the indicator on and slowed even more as he made the turn into a little driveway. The headlights briefly illuminated the For Sale sign as he drove by.

'What's this place?' Maggie asked, a crease running along her brow. Nothing some Botox wouldn't have taken care of, but where she was going, no amount of chemicals would make her look better. Well, formaldehyde might for a little while.

He beamed a smile at her, slipping into character. His white teeth shone through his designer stubble. It was one of his most distinguishing features, a girlfriend had once said. This gold-digger hadn't told him anything, but to give her her due, she had squealed with delight when she saw the gold credit card slip out of his wallet. It had been stolen and he would never try to use it, but he made sure they saw it, his thumb covering the rightful owner's name.

'This is ours!' he shouted, not quite loud enough to scare her but with exuberant excitement.

'Ours? What do you mean, *ours?*' she said, her voice rising.

He looked over at her in the darkness of the car. 'This place is a stepping stone to our future. After my divorce, we can sell this place and get something special. But here, we can stay out of sight and have all the privacy we need. Do you like it?' *Please say you like it, you ungrateful bitch.*

'Of course I like it,' she said when she saw the small cottage appearing in the headlight beams. It was like something out of an oil painting, like the ones on the calendar her mother got every year.

'It's dark,' she said, her smile wavering.

He gave a small laugh, which saved him from unleashing the sarcasm. *Of course it's fucking dark. There are no lights on and we're in the middle of nowhere.*

'There are lights we can leave on outside and I'm going to have a security company come out and fix some cameras.'

'Oh, that's terrific, Peter,' she said, just as the car triggered the automatic light above the front door and the detached garage off to one side.

'As if by magic!' he said.

The headlights swept in front of the house. Another For Sale sign was stuck outside, in case you were daft and hadn't noticed the one by the road and just happened to drive along somebody's drive.

The property was bordered by thick trees, which afforded even more privacy. Trees sheltered the garage too. In theory, there could be somebody hiding round the back of there now, waiting to jump out, but by God, it would be the last thing he ever did.

Nobody jumped out.

'This place looks like something out of a fairy tale,' Maggie enthused, and Peter looked across at her for a moment, thinking she was taking the piss.

'I'm glad you like it,' he said, seeing that she was genuinely taken with the place.

'Don't keep a lady waiting,' Maggie said, already

pulling on the door handle and opening the door. The cold night air rushed in and Peter was out in a flash, pulling his leather gloves tighter. The fact it was winter made it easy to keep the gloves on when he was driving.

'Before we go in,' he said, 'I just want to check the garage. See if it's big enough for the Beemer.' He smiled towards the old 3 Series. It was her car. He had told her that friends of his wife might see them driving about in his car so it would be best if they used hers. Little did she know he wasn't married.

'I thought you said this place was ours?'

'I did.'

'But you don't know if the car will fit in?' She looked at him like he was stupid for a second.

'When I came to look at it, the estate agent had parked her car in front of one of the garage doors. I parked next to her, and I was so excited about the house, I forgot to ask how big the garage was inside.'

Maggie laughed. 'Sometimes I wonder why your first wife put up with you for so long.'

Peter smiled with his mouth closed and clamped his teeth together. Maybe he should just do her in the fucking car now and be done with it. He controlled himself, wanting to stick to the plan. Once you started to deviate, there were variables you couldn't control. He had left the car running. Last thing he wanted was to be stuck out here. He looked at Maggie illuminated by the headlights and thought it was a good image to remember her by.

He turned and walked over to the garage door and pretended to fiddle with the door lock. 'Crap, it's locked. I thought the agent said it would be left open since there's nothing in it to steal. Give me a minute, honey. I want to put the Beemer inside.'

'Okay, but don't be long.'

Peter slipped out of the headlight beams and went round the back of the garage. Maggie stood in the cold air, her breath blowing out like steam. She stamped her feet, trying to get some warmth into them.

The garage door slowly started to open up. No lights came on, but instead she heard Peter yelling.

'Christ, I've fallen, Maggie. I think I've sprained my ankle.'

Maggie's heart skipped a beat as she walked towards the garage opening, trying not to slip on the snowy driveway.

'Where are you?' she shouted.

'In here. Behind the boxes. My leg's stuck behind something.'

'Oh no, Peter, hold on, I'm coming. I'll call for an ambulance.'

'No, I don't need an ambulance. I just need you, precious. Please help me.'

'Oh Lord. I'm coming for you, my darling. Just hold on.'

The garage was dark and filled with old pieces of furniture and boxes stacked one on top of another. The smell was awful, like some dead person's attic. She stepped in, her phone in her hand, the light on the back cutting through the gloom. The light from the car didn't make it into here, more's the pity.

'Peter, where are you?'

No reply.

'Peter, talk to me.' She shone the light about, illuminating smelly old furniture that would make a good starter for a bonfire.

She walked further in, squeezing between two piles of boxes. 'Peter?' she said, her voice now sounding like a hoarse whisper. 'Where are you?'

'Right behind you,' he said.

Maggie turned round and saw Peter wearing an old leather apron. He had a visor on his head. He was smiling at her behind the clear face shield.

She was about to scream when he brought the knife down.

THIRTEEN

Bracken closed the lounge door behind him and Natalie sat on the couch along from the chairs. 'You don't mind if I switch on the TV, do you?' she asked.

'Go right ahead. I can go to my room, give you peace,' he said.

She looked at him, her smile gone. 'Don't go on my account. I just wanted to get out of my room for a bit. Stay and watch some mindless drivel with me. I like watching the soaps. They make my life positively exciting. They make me feel like my life isn't so bad after all.'

Bracken got up from his chair and sat down on the opposite end of the couch, carrying his beer bottle with him. He'd had enough of the hooligan juice for one night. Sticking to beer meant there was a fifty-fifty chance of him getting up before lunchtime tomorrow.

'Get you one?' he said, holding up the bottle. Then he felt like he was in a nightclub trying to get some daft lassie to dance with him.

'No, thanks. I don't drink much these days. I'll have an orange juice, if you're offering.'

Bracken looked at her.

'You don't know where my uncle Bob keeps the beer and the orange, do you?' she said, looking back at him.

'Nope. You should be a detective.'

'You stay there and I'll go and get them.'

'You are a good lass after all.'

She laughed as she got up and left the room to get the drinks. She came back a few minutes later. 'Uncle Bob said just go through to the kitchen and help yourself. You put some there after all, he said. And they have two big fridges.'

'Cheers.'

The soap started and Bracken had to admit that he had watched more *SpongeBob* in the past year than any soap. Sometimes he just needed some mindless cartoon to distract him from the horrors of real life.

'You like living here?' he said eventually.

'Yes. You?'

'Bob and Mary have a nice place here.'

'If you like that sort of thing.'

They watched some TV in silence, Bracken starting to feel awkward.

He nodded and drank some of the beer. Natalie was going to be a tough nut to crack, conversation wise, and he didn't think he had the strength to deal with it. One beer, then he'd fuck off up the stairs and look at the pattern on the wallpaper. Maybe that would have more conversation in it. He didn't think Natalie would have much success at speed dating.

'I'm sorry,' she said to him.

'That's okay. I've known plenty of women who only drink orange juice.'

'No, I meant...' Then she smiled and nodded. 'Touché. Sometimes I just get fed up of answering the same questions, but that's mostly from the tourists. You're different.'

'Different how?'

'You're one of us now. No disrespect to Mary and Bob, but once you get settled here, it's like being in an episode of *The Twilight Zone*. It's like we can never leave.'

Answers rattled through Bracken's brain, but none of them seemed appropriate. He knew why the old couple were here, but he didn't know Natalie's story.

'What line of work are you in?' he asked.

'I fill shelves in Tesco along the road in Corstorphine. Just until I win the lottery.'

He tried to think of another work-related thing to say, but 'must be exciting tossing loaves of bread onto a shelf' didn't sound like the proper segue into an in-depth talk on life on the supermarket floor.

'Why are you living here?' he asked, feeling tiredness creeping in and not in the mood to play games anymore. 'If it's not a personal question.'

'Well, it is a personal question, isn't it?'

Jesus. Still with the games.

'Sorry, I was just making conversation.' He drank his beer, not feeling in the slightest bit sorry.

'I know. Christ, sometimes I get too defensive.' She sipped some of the orange juice. 'Didn't Uncle Bob tell you about me?'

'He never said a word.' *And now I know that if he ever does try to tell me about somebody in the future, I'll kill the bastard where he stands.*

Natalie made eye contact with him, like some detective in an interview room looking at his body language.

'I didn't always fill shelves for a living.'

He wasn't about to fall into the trap of asking where she had started before that, so he kept quiet.

'I was a doctor. A GP.'

That got his attention. He looked at her like she was having him on, like when people said they were something like an urban rejuvenation engineer when they were really a street sweeper.

'No, really, I was.'

'Of course you were.' Bracken drank some more beer, wondering if she was dangerous. Tired or not, he would wrestle her to the floor and cuff her, if that's what it took.

Natalie grabbed the remote and aimed it at the TV, muting the sound. 'You know something, that's the first time I've told anybody what I was before working at Tesco. And your reaction is exactly why.' She turned away from him, like she was offended.

'Oh, God, I'm sorry.' He was going to put a hand on her shoulder but snapped it back. That was the last thing he needed, a gesture being mistaken for something it wasn't.

She turned back to him and smiled. 'Relax, Sean. I was kidding. You're not the first one I've told and I'm not some nutter who needs help and who goes around making up stories.'

Again with the fucking games. 'You're a good actress, though.' He finished the beer and stood up. 'Well, I'll bid you goodnight, *Doctor.*'

'Don't say it like that. Ugh. Sometimes my sense of humour gets me in trouble. Please, sit back down.'

He looked at her, wondering if she had a pair of scissors hiding down the side of the settee.

'I'll get another beer.'

He left and returned with his bottle and a little bottle of OJ mixer.

'Cheers,' Natalie said as he handed it over and sat back down. There was nothing to indicate she was holding scissors. 'I'm sorry, Sean. That was a mixture of bitterness and anger rather than humour.'

'I'm not thin-skinned.'

'I know, but I could see I pushed it too far. So let me tell you the life story of Natalie Hogan. It all started when I was a little girl.' She smiled at him. 'Christ, I'm doing it again. God, you can tell I haven't been in the company of a man in a long time.'

'Just relax, Natalie. Tell me what you want to tell me and leave out the rest.'

'Right. I was a GP, and my husband and I took our son for a holiday in the Highlands. We went hiking, and me being the stupid cow that I am, I pushed myself too hard. I fell down a hill. Not too far, but I put my right hand out and landed hard. I tore through several layers of my rotator cuff. I was in so much pain and needed surgery. Which I eventually got. I couldn't work and the doc I was seeing told me he would have to cut back on the painkillers he was prescribing me. You can guess what came next, can't you?'

'You got hooked.'

'Oh yes. Not only that – I started writing out my own prescriptions. And I got caught. I barely escaped prison, and I lost my job and got struck off. My husband left me and took our little boy with him. Because I started buying painkillers on the streets. He won sole custody of Rory and I get to see him every other weekend. I can't afford my own place to take him to, but he's been here a few times. Mary and Bob fuss over him and he likes them.'

'I'm sorry to hear that, Natalie. Not about Bob and Mary fussing over the wee yin, I mean.'

'Don't be. It was my own fault. Nobody forced me to buy drugs from a street pusher.'

'Christ, you needed help. Sounds to me like the system let you down.'

She drank some of the orange. 'I'm hoping this won't be forever, but you know...' She didn't finish the sentence.

'How old is Rory?'

'He's eight now. Handsome wee boy. God, I miss him so much.'

'Is your husband a doctor?' Bracken asked.

'Ex-husband. After he got custody, he filed for divorce. Two years later, it was granted, and he had already moved on by then. When the divorce was finalised, he married his girlfriend. They've been husband and wife for over a year now. And no, he isn't a doctor.'

Bracken drank some more beer and waited.

'He's the Scottish justice minister,' Natalie said. And then unmuted the TV.

FOURTEEN

Bracken expected to smell death and disinfectant in the city mortuary, but what met him instead was the smell of bacon rolls.

Dr Pamela Green was wiping tomato sauce from her mouth when he stopped at the open doorway to her office and knocked on the doorframe.

'Sean! Just in time. We got you a bacon roll in case you hadn't had any breakfast.' She turned to the young woman sitting in the other chair. 'You remember head mortuary tech Chaz Cullen?'

'Pam, it was yesterday. He hasn't got the attention span of a goldfish.' Chaz smiled at him. 'Have you?'

'I'm sorry, what was the question again?'

Pam laughed. 'You'll fit in here just fine, Sean Bracken.'

'Good to meet you again, Chaz.' Bracken looked at

the young woman with the dark hair and wondered if the purple stripes were natural. She smiled at him, so he thought he would reserve judgement on whether he would think of her as Chav instead of Chaz.

'You too, Sean. Or do you prefer the great unwashed to address you by rank?' she asked him and took a bite of the roll.

Pam was holding out a ball of tinfoil, which he assumed was keeping the roll warm. He stepped forward and took it. 'Thank you.' He looked at Chaz. 'Sean's fine.'

'The reason I ask is old Billy Bunter...I mean Burton; he only wanted to be addressed by rank. I drew the line at saluting him, of course, but I know that one day soon we'll be opening him up on one of the tables. He likes to tell us he works out, but there's a fat man inside just dying to get out. If you'll pardon the pun.'

Bracken raised his eyebrows as he unwrapped the roll. He'd only had a small bowl of cornflakes for breakfast at the guest house; after turning his alarm off, the 'extra five minutes' he'd promised himself had turned into an hour.

'Like us, he's clogging his arteries with bacon rolls, but he goes the extra mile and adds doughnuts,' Chaz explained. 'Have you seen the size of him? His talking scales shout, *One at a time, please!*'

'I love coming here,' Bracken said, sitting on a chair as Pam got up and poured some coffees from the kettle, which had been chuntering away on a table in a corner. 'You get a decent roll, then you're told it's going to kill you. Next you'll be telling me cigarettes are bad for you.'

'There's a new report out that says alcohol might not be the best tonic either,' Pam said. 'Milk in your coffee?'

Bracken nodded as he took a bite of his roll. 'No sugar,' he said, and it sounded like Klingon with the food in his mouth.

'We're all agreed that food, smoking and drinking are bad for us?' Pam said, handing out the mugs of coffee.

'And here we are adding caffeine to the list,' Bracken said, raising his mug in salute.

Chaz clinked mugs with him like they were champagne glasses. 'Don't worry, one day they'll invent a pill we can take instead of eating and it will have everything we need to survive.'

'I thought that was E?' Bracken said.

'I wouldn't know, Chief Inspector.' She drank some of the coffee. 'Oops, sorry, I only use a copper's title when I'm trying not to incriminate myself.'

'You haven't taken any of that muck, have you?' Pam said, sitting down with a worried look on her face.

Chaz laughed. 'Of course not, Mum. I was just wanting to see if our new friend would squirm or read me my rights.'

'And he did neither. I'm glad he's here to stay.'

'Me too. I could get used to him coming here all the time.' Chaz smiled at Bracken.

'Give over, he's old enough to be your dad.'

'I can hear you,' Bracken said, finishing his roll. He balled up the foil and put it on the desk. 'But Pam's right; I have a daughter not much younger than you look.'

'A girl can try.'

Bracken hoped his cheeks weren't going red. He drank some more coffee.

'Billy Burton called me this morning and asked me to come along to get the post-mortem report,' he said.

'On a Saturday too. Did you pull the short straw?' Chaz asked.

'Time is of the essence. I'm just a small cog in this big machine. A woman's dead, and the bastard who took her life is probably sitting with his feet up, eating a bacon roll.'

The women looked at him. 'Where were you on Thursday night?' Pam asked.

'Sorry to disappoint you, but I was in the pub having some farewell drinks with a few of my friends.'

'Damn. I thought I was in the presence of a killer

and was going to show him some of my best Krav Maga moves,' Chaz said.

'I thought Krav Maga was a chocolate cake?' Bracken said.

'Your nickname's going to be Hardened Arteries when you come in here in a body bag,' she replied.

Pam got up from behind her desk and walked over to a filing cabinet and pulled out a file. 'I think we're far from being a paperless office,' she said, handing him the report. 'Toxicology won't be back until God knows when, but it was just as I'd suspected: cause of death was cutting her carotid. She has seven smaller stab wounds, but none of them would have been enough to kill her. She would have been in a hell of a lot of pain, obviously, but none were fatal.'

Bracken read through the file for a few minutes before looking at the doctor. 'The eyes were removed post-mortem?'

'They were indeed.' Pam looked at him. 'Just like Ailsa Connolly's victims.'

'I'd forgotten about her,' Chaz asked, drinking more coffee.

Bracken looked up from the file. 'You know our Ailsa?'

Chaz nodded and popped the last of the roll into her mouth.

'She was sort of instrumental in guiding me. I woke

up one morning and told myself I would go to uni and get a good degree and get myself a decent career.'

'But you ended up here instead,' Bracken said, his eyes going back to the paperwork.

Chaz sucked air into her mouth through her teeth. 'Pam warned me about you.'

'She only met me yesterday.'

'Exactly. Met you for five minutes and that was all she needed. He takes no prisoners, she said. Now I see what she meant.'

'I also shoot from the hip,' Bracken said, smiling at her.

'Whatever that means.' Chaz balled up her napkin and fired it at the wastepaper basket at the side of Pam's desk. It missed by a mile.

'You weren't on the basketball team at uni, I take it?' Bracken added.

'I'll give you a tenner if you get yours in from there.'

Bracken picked up the ball of silver foil and fired it straight into the bin.

'That's bloody cheating,' Chaz said.

'How?' Bracken asked.

'It just is. Now I won't be able to go out on the lash tonight because Shaq there bounced it into the bin first time.'

'Keep your money. Buy me a drink next time I see

you in the pub,' Bracken answered, reading more of the file.

'How do you know which pub I drink in?'

He looked at her. 'I'm a copper, remember? You go out drinking with the others in here, maybe sometimes on a Friday after work. Or during the week. And if that's the case, it would be at the Inn on the Mile.'

Chaz paused for a second. 'Now just hold on a gosh darn moment there, Captain Smartypants. How do you know it isn't the Mitre we drink in across the road from there? Or the Royal Mile next door to that?'

'I told you; I'm good at my job.'

Chaz's mouth hung open. Then she turned to Pam. 'Can you believe this guy? Sherlock can't hold a candle to him.'

'Either that or I mentioned to him yesterday that we drink there,' Pam said.

Chaz made a *disappointed parent* look and shook her head. 'I should make you go to your room for telling me such fibs, young man.'

Bracken smiled. 'You know I'm going to be in there after Christmas, so bring that moth farm you call a purse. And before you ask, Dr Green didn't tell me you're a tight wad. I saw the receipt for the rolls on her desk in front of her. When you buy something, you usually put the receipt away in a bag or pocket – unless somebody else is paying. Then you give them the receipt. Therefore, you got the rolls, but Pam paid for them.'

Pam shrugged. 'He is a *chief* inspector. That's why they pay him the big bucks.'

'Point taken,' said Chaz. 'But have you deduced why somebody would kill our guest and then take her eyes out? Just like Miss Connolly.'

Bracken looked at her. 'Not *Miss* anymore. She got married a week ago.'

'Shut the front door.' Both women sat up.

'You genuinely didn't know?'

Pam looked at Chaz. 'There seems to have been a breakdown in our gossip chain.' Then to Bracken, 'No, we didn't know. Tell us more.'

'I don't have all the details, but apparently it was to some doctor she's known for a long time. Robert Marshall.'

'He must be daft to marry her,' Chaz said.

'He's a psychologist like her, so I don't think he's too daft.' He closed the file and tapped it. 'Have you read the reports from six years ago when Ailsa killed those other people?' he asked Pam.

'I have. She was really sick. God knows how she got transferred to the Royal Edinburgh.'

'She denied killing some of those people, though, didn't she?' Chaz said.

'She did. She openly admitted to killing some but not all.'

'The kids,' Pam said. 'She said she didn't kill the kids.'

'Do you believe her?' Bracken asked.

'No. I hope she rots in hell. Why? Do you?'

Before Bracken could answer, his phone rang in his pocket. He took it out and answered it. Listened to the caller on the other end. 'Okay. I'll be there as soon as. I'm down at the mortuary just now. I'll leave in a minute.' He hung up.

'Got to go, eh?' Chaz said. 'Hope to see you soon.'

'You'll see me sooner than you think; we just got a shout. Dead female in a house near Ratho.'

Just then, Pamela Green's phone rang.

Bracken stood up and put a hand on Chaz's shoulder as he passed. 'See you soon. Oh, and one more thing.'

'What's that?'

'The Harlem Globetrotters called. They want their ball back.'

FIFTEEN

Bracken relied on the satnav in his car. Although it had been a while since he had been in Edinburgh, he remembered the roads well, and he didn't recall ever having been through Ratho or along the surrounding country roads. He let the female voice take him from the A71 down Hermiston House Road, which looked like a country lane built for horse carriages back in the day.

Bracken had called Sullivan but got no answer. Now he called Charlie Nelson, asking for specific directions to the crime scene.

'Come down Hermiston House Road and we're right at the T-junction. You'd have to be a real spoon to miss it. I mean, not that you would miss it, sir.'

The cheeky wee bastard started to babble at that point, so Bracken put him out of his misery and hung up, promising himself that if the young DC spoke to him like that again, he really would put the little fucker out of his misery.

The council trucks obviously didn't see this road as a priority and had given it a quick once-over, but not recently. Snow had come down and stuck up two fingers at the yellow truck's effort to move it along. Bracken felt the back of the car slide out and corrected it. He was sure Nelson and the satnav were taking the piss, telling him to come down this road.

It looked like the road ahead disappeared into thin air, but then he realised it took a ninety-degree turn. He slowed the car down, dropping a couple of gears, listening to the engine protest. Then, when he turned the steering wheel, the car refused to play for a moment and decided it wanted to go through a wall instead, but Bracken was having none of it and took the car round the corner and over a little stone bridge and carried on.

'See that scrap merchant along the road?' he said to the car. 'You're fucking next.'

A patrol car was waiting at the end of the narrow road. Bracken pulled over to the side, got out onto the snow-covered road and showed his ID to the uniform.

Charlie Nelson was standing by the entrance to the driveway of the house.

'You found it then, sir?'

'Aye, the flashing blue lights on top of the car were a dead giveaway. Is Sullivan here?'

'Yes, sir. He's in there with a woman who looks like she just saw a ghost.'

'Probably worse than a ghost, eh?' Bracken's breath was grabbed by the frigid air and taken away.

They walked onto the driveway, where a blue Nissan sat. Nelson showed Bracken into the garage at the side of the house, where Sullivan and Izzie were waiting while the forensics crew were doing their thing.

The detached building was filled with all sorts of clutter, the bulk of it old furniture, but some of it had been moved so the dead woman was the centrepiece and couldn't be missed.

'What have we got here?' Bracken asked Sullivan, who was looking down at the form of a young female.

'She doesn't appear to have been sexually assaulted at least,' Sullivan said. 'But she's been stabbed and had her throat slit. And of course –'

'The eyes are gone,' Bracken said, finishing the DI's sentence for him.

'Correct.'

A white-suited man stood up and walked over to them. 'Nasty.'

Bracken wasn't sure if the man meant him or the corpse.

'The sick bastard left her here like a piece of meat,' the man added.

'I don't believe we've been introduced,' Bracken said, waiting for Sullivan to do the honours.

'This is Kevin Morris, head of forensics. DCI Bracken, new head of MIT West.'

'I've seen you around, a long time ago, mind, but your face is familiar,' Morris said. He was a man in his fifties who had long ago given up on any attempt to eat healthily.

'I was here a few years back. Anything stick out?' Bracken nodded towards the girl.

'I would say she was killed here, given the amount of blood we have on the floor.'

Bracken looked around him. 'This is a bit isolated, this place. Who found her?'

'An estate agent, Olive Yates. She had been sent an email from a woman called Maggie Scott asking if she could view this property this morning. The agent turned up and saw the body in the garage.'

'That's her car out there?'

'It is,' Sullivan replied. 'She said when she arrived here, there were tyre marks in the snow, so she just drove along them.'

'Obliterating the other tyres' tread pattern,' Morris said.

'Would I be correct in assuming that the victim is

Maggie Scott, the woman who emailed for an appointment?' Bracken said.

'Yes, you would. We checked her driving licence.'

'We need to find out what kind of car she drove, if it's still at her residence and if anybody knew where she was going last night, or yesterday. Time of death will have to be determined, but she doesn't look like she's been here for days. I could be wrong, but –'

'You're not,' Pamela Green said, walking into the garage. 'From what I can see, she hasn't been dead that long. I'll be able to determine more exactly later, but it doesn't look like days.'

'It's been cold and that would have slowed decomposition,' Morris added.

'Hello again, Chief Inspector,' Chaz said, smiling at Bracken. 'Long time no see.'

'That's true. Maybe we should all get together for a bacon roll sometime.'

They turned to look at Izzie as she came to the edge of the garage door. 'It's no more than two days,' she said.

'You got a medical degree?' Bracken asked her.

'No, sir. The agent showed a man this property on Thursday morning and there was no body lying in the middle of the garage floor.'

'He got a name, this customer?'

'Peter Wallis.'

'I'll let you get on with the exam, Doctor. Let's go and talk to this agent again, Jimmy.'

Chaz smiled at Bracken as he passed and he afforded her the slightest of smiles, something a Cheshire Cat would have scoffed at.

He led the way out into the cold air again. 'I'm assuming she's in the house?'

'She is, sir,' Izzie replied and they all traipsed over to the front door of the stone building.

Inside, a woman of around forty was sitting on a settee with a female uniform next to her. Bracken knew somebody somewhere would think this sexist, but he knew that women were far superior to men in most ways and certainly when it came to showing comfort and compassion. A few men he knew would do well to learn from some of his female colleagues.

'I'm DCI Bracken,' he said to the woman, who had been dabbing at her eyes. 'I'm in charge of this investigation, Mrs Yates.'

'This is awful. I thought he was still here and was going to kill me too.' She started shaking and dabbed at her eyes again.

Bracken didn't think this woman was involved, but he noticed that nobody turned their back on her. Her innocence still had to be established. Not many people had forgotten Ailsa Connolly. Except maybe Chaz.

'Can you tell us more about this man, Peter Wallis, who you showed the property to on Thursday?'

Olive looked at him, as if seeing his face would bring up the image of the man she had been alone with and who, in her mind, might have chopped her up into a thousand pieces.

'He was average build. Not sure what hair colour because he was wearing a woollen hat and he didn't take it off. He had one of those half-beard things, like when men don't shave for a few days and they think it makes them God's gift to women. He was wearing a dark coat.'

'What did his voice sound like? Accent? Anything special about it, like a lisp?'

She shook her head. 'He spoke like somebody from Edinburgh. But from a posh part, like Morningside, not Niddrie. He wore sunglasses all the time, even when we came in here.'

'Let me guess: he was wearing gloves and didn't take them off?'

'Yes. He never really touched anything, like most people do. Opening cupboards and things like that. He didn't seem as interested in the house as he was in the garage. He said he had an old classic car and the garage had to be just right. He wasn't bothered by the junk in there as I told him the previous owner would have it cleared out.'

'What kind of car was he driving?'

'A white BMW Three Series.'

'I don't suppose you got the number plate?' Bracken asked.

Olive nodded. 'Yes, I did.'

SIXTEEN

Bracken turned to Sullivan and a look passed between them; the first person in history to get the number plate of an alleged killer.

Olive took her phone out. 'I took it when he wasn't looking. Some of my colleagues let prospective buyers know they're doing it, but I didn't want to offend this man. He was genuinely enthusiastic about the place and not a lot of people have been lately, so I switched the sound off on my phone, took the photo and sent it to a friend in my office. Just so we would have a record. You can't be too careful nowadays, and for good reason.'

She held out the phone for Bracken to take and he looked at the photo of the white saloon car. He showed it to Sullivan, who took his own phone out and took a photo of the photo. He then stepped away and went into the hallway to have control run the number.

Bracken handed the phone back to Olive. 'I don't suppose you got a photo of Wallis?'

'No. I'm not that brazen.'

A few minutes later, Sullivan came back into the room. 'The car belongs to our victim, Maggie Scott. He was using it.'

'Right.' Bracken's tone said that he shouldn't have been surprised. This killer was clever. He asked Olive, 'Do you have the numbers Wallis and Miss Scott called from?'

'It was all through email. He sent me one on Wednesday, and then yesterday Miss Scott sent me one telling me her boyfriend was the one who had been shown round on Thursday. Oh, I didn't mention that, did I?'

You most certainly did fucking not, Bracken thought, but he just gave his best smile, the one he would use to cover the groan that might have come out in its place.

'Don't worry, this is a stressful time. At least you remembered. Let me get this straight: Peter Wallis emailed you wanting to view the property and he turned up on Thursday. Then yesterday Maggie Scott emailed you, informing you that Peter Wallis was her boyfriend and he'd had a look around and now she wanted to. You arranged a time for her to meet you here today. Does that sound about right?'

'Yes.'

'I'd like to read those emails if you don't mind. Maybe our tech guys could get the IP they were sent from.'

'Of course. Here, I have my iPad with me. You can read the emails on there.'

Bracken watched as once again Olive dived into her bag, wondering if she was navigating past the kitchen sink to get the iPad. Then it surfaced. She opened it up, got to her emails and opened the one from Wallis.

Bracken read it. The message didn't give any incriminating clues, but it did give the email address it had come from: Maggie Scott's, *maggiescott92*.

'What's Maggie's date of birth?' he asked Sullivan, who took out his phone and looked at the photo he'd taken of her licence. Bracken had assumed his DI had taken this shot.

'September sixth, nineteen ninety-two. She's twenty-eight.'

'Her email address is her name and year of birth. And Wallis used it to send the email. He either has access to her computer or to her email login. Find out which.'

'Maybe it's both,' Sullivan said.

'Could be. Check her phone too, see if anything was sent from there.' Bracken didn't know all the ins and outs of how to send email from a phone but didn't want to show his ignorance.

'I recognise your company from the For Sale sign outside,' he said to Olive. 'You were selling a farm near the Pentlands. Do you represent a lot of country properties?'

'In this day and age, we represent everything. The market's still a bit tough, so we had to diversify.'

'Right, Mrs Yates, we'll make sure a police officer takes you home, or at least escorts you in your car if you feel up to driving. If you see anything suspicious near your house or work, give us a call. Treble nine if you have to.'

'Thank you.'

Bracken and Sullivan left the living room.

'Where did Maggie Scott live?' Bracken asked.

'Her address is in Barnton.'

'Find out where she worked and see if anybody saw this Wallis character. And run that name through the database and see how many people with that name live around here, then throw the net wider if you have to.'

Just then a car skidded into the side of the road and the driver's door flew open. They watched as Superintendent Billy Burton climbed out and slammed the door shut.

'In the name of Christ, who suggested coming down that wee road there?' he said, striding over to the two men. 'I nearly went through a fucking wall. That wee arsehole Nelson told me everybody was coming down that way.'

'It's a bit tricky, right enough,' Bracken said.

'Tricky? My arse nearly ate the seat back there. That laddie's going to be standing outside a school directing traffic next week. And by God he'll be the one on call on Christmas Day.' He blew out a breath as if he was trying to get his heart rate down. 'Give me an update.'

'A young woman, killed in the detached garage over there,' Bracken said. 'Same way as the other victim.'

'Jesus. What do you know about the victim? Any connection to the first?'

'Still working on it, sir; we're going to her address. It seems a man she knew came to look over the place on Thursday, then the victim arranged a viewing for today, but when the estate agent turned up, she found the woman murdered.'

The sun was coming out now and starting to bounce off the snow.

'How do you know he knew her?'

'The request for an appointment was made from the victim's email, and the victim told the agent he was her boyfriend.'

'I wonder if it's the same man who made an appointment to go and see the farm yesterday. Check the emails, see where they came from.'

'One of the DS's is on it now, sir,' Sullivan said.

'Good. Keep me in the loop. The commander is breathing down my neck, wanting updates all the fucking time. And if I waited on you lot to update me, I'd have reached retirement age. But don't go baking me a cake just yet. This old dog is going to kick this killer's arse when he gets hold of him.'

Bracken couldn't imagine Burton kicking anybody's arse, but he kept quiet.

'You think Ailsa Connolly's got anything to do with this?' Burton asked.

'Maybe she inspired somebody to use her MO,' Bracken said. 'It wouldn't be the first time.'

'I want you to go and talk to her husband. That quack – what's his name again?'

'Robert Marshall.'

'Aye, him. I wonder why he married her? I mean, they knew each other a long time ago, but why would he want to get hitched to her?'

'It happens more than you'd think,' Sullivan said.

'Is that how you met your wife?' Burton said.

'No, I met her on a Thai bride site. Sucky, Fucky, Five Bucky. Except I bought her and had her shipped over.'

'You know, if you keep talking pish like that, I won't believe you when you do have something half-intelligent to say.'

'My point is,' said Sullivan, 'there are weirdos who marry prisoners, of both sexes. Since Marshall worked with her years ago, maybe he had a thing for her back then but couldn't do anything about it. And for some reason, he wanted to marry her, even if he couldn't be with her.'

'Find out where he lives and go talk to him.'

'Will do,' Bracken said.

They stood in silence for a second.

'Well, don't let me keep you.' Burton shrugged his shoulders up as clouds drifted in again, killing the sun.

They watched as the older detective walked over to the garage, where the forensics crew were working along with Pamela Green. Chaz was nowhere to be seen.

Charlie Nelson walked out of the front door with Izzie and looked over at the entrance. 'Crap. Is Burton here?' he said.

'It's Detective Superintendent to you,' Bracken said. 'Did you deliberately send him down that fucking side road, just like you did me?'

'It's the shortest way,' Nelson said lamely.

'We barely made it in one piece. I bet you nearly ended up upside down in a field too.'

'Me? I didn't come down that way. I came past the scrapyard.'

Little bastard. 'But you made me come down that way. If I'd wrecked my fucking car...'

'You asked for the quickest way. So did Superintendent Burton.'

There was no faulting the boy's logic. 'Are you special, son?'

'Privacy laws prevent me from answering that question, sir. My mum thinks I'm special, though.'

'I bet she fucking does.' Bracken shook his head. Then turned to Izzie. 'Take this miscreant and go to the estate agent's office and see what other properties like this and the farm they have on the books. And have somebody trace the IP address that the emails were sent from. If it was a laptop, it might have hooked into somebody else's Wi-Fi.'

'Yes, sir,' Izzie said.

She walked away with Nelson, scolding him for talking to Bracken like that.

'He's a good lad, really,' said Sullivan, 'but a bit misguided at times. Works like a Trojan, though; that's why we keep him in MIT.'

117

'Isn't a Trojan a computer virus?' said Bracken. 'Worms its way in and a right bastard to get rid of?'

'I think so.'

'Then that seems fitting.'

They'd started walking towards Bracken's car when Burton shouted at them from the garage. They turned back.

'Sean, I want you to go and interview Ailsa Connolly. Tomorrow. We have to give those officious bastards twenty-four hours' notice.'

'You think she might be of use to us?'

'If somebody's copying her technique, she might be able to give us some insight. But go alone. She might clam up if anybody else is there with you. No offence, Sullivan.'

'None taken.'

'I'll give them a call,' Bracken said.

'I already did,' Burton told him. 'Any time after twelve is good.'

Bracken looked at his watch; 11.19. 'Twenty-four hours and forty minutes until I get to meet the woman who once tried to kill me.'

'Yep. Give her my regards. Tell her I hope she rots in hell. But don't say that bit until you're about to leave. It wouldn't do to get on her bad side *before* you questioned her.'

Burton trudged through the snow and got back into his car.

They heard footsteps coming up behind them in the snow and Bracken turned round first. Chaz, her cheeks rosy. 'Sean, can I have a word?'

'My car's out there. Go and get her running, Jimmy.' He handed the keys to Sullivan, who walked away.

'You're either feeling the cold or you drink early in the day,' Bracken said to Chaz.

'Listen to Coco the Clown. You'd do well to warm your conker there, Chief Inspector.'

'Now that we've slagged each other off, I have to be going.'

She reached a hand out as he made to leave and grabbed the sleeve of his coat. 'A few of us are going for a drink tonight. If you'd like to join us?'

Bracken thought about it. 'How many're going?'

She looked at him. 'Well, me and Pam, and Nick and Ed, the other mortuary assistants.'

'I don't know the others. They might feel awkward around me.'

'You're like a wee boy going to a new school for the first time.'

'Now you're being ridiculous.'

'First time for everything.' She laughed. 'Come on. It'll be fun. Have a drink and a laugh.'

Bracken smiled. 'How old are you?'

'Age is just a number.'

'Listen, I'm not knocking you back, and I might join the lot of you some other time, but tonight I need to talk to my daughter. Maybe I'll get there.'

'Okay, that's cool. Coco.'

'What's Chaz short for?' he asked.

'Me to know and you to find out,' she said, laughing, as she walked away, leaving Bracken feeling like he should be flattered that a younger woman wanted to have a drink with him, but actually feeling like this was wrong on so many levels.

Sullivan had started the car and the air inside was warm, if not in competition with a furnace just yet.

'She's nice,' Sullivan said.

'Who? The car?' Bracken said, connecting his seatbelt.

'Chaz.'

'I know. She's also young.'

'I wish younger women would give me the come-on,' Sullivan complained as Bracken drove away, heading back along the road, just not the one he'd come down.

'You're married, son,' Bracken admonished. 'You should be happy you have a nice wife and two kids.'

'I never said my wife was nice. I just said I had one.'

Bracken looked at him before picking up speed.

'Who am I kidding?' Sullivan said with a sigh. 'She is nice, and I love her. But now and again, it would be nice to have my ego inflated just a few PSI above normal.'

'You should be content with what you have.'

'Don't get me wrong, I am. But when I see an old guy getting the come-on from a younger woman...well, that's just a kick in the goolies.'

'What old man?' Bracken asked.

'Oh, another older man – not you, boss.'

'Cheeky bastard. Just get the address into that satnav and less of your bloody lip.'

SEVENTEEN

Again, the satnav directed Bracken to his destination – a mere ten minutes as the crow flies but considerably more by road. It was a straightforward run, hitting the Edinburgh Bypass and then Maybury Road and across the intersection. The sky was painted grey again, and it was snowing by the time they got to Barnton Brae, off Barnton Avenue West.

'Old money down here, but they still find some open spaces to build houses on. The Royal Burgess golf club will be next. There's some developer somewhere foaming at the mouth, just aching to build big houses on the fairways.'

'I wouldn't mind living down here,' Sullivan said.

'You and me both, son. Just not in the same house, you understand.'

The house they were looking for was huge, with

high hedges round it. And a gate blocking their way. There was an intercom on top of a post near the gate. Bracken rolled the window down and pressed the button.

'Can I help you?' a female voice said.

'Police. We need to come in and speak to somebody.'

There was hesitation for a moment before the woman spoke again. 'Can you hold your warrant card up to the camera above the button, please?'

Bracken obliged and held it up. They heard a click and the metal gate slid sideways. It looked like it could stop a runaway truck.

'Who wants to live like this?' Sullivan said.

'You just said a minute ago *you* wanted to,' Bracken said, rolling his window back up. 'Make up your bloody mind.'

He pulled the car forward and parked beside a Jaguar and a Mercedes four-wheel drive. Snow started falling again as they walked across the wide driveway. It had been shovelled only recently and Bracken could feel the rock salt crunching under his boots.

A young woman answered the door. She pulled her wool sweater around herself as she stood in the vestibule.

'What's this about?' she said.

'Mrs Scott?' Bracken asked as he and Sullivan

showed her their warrant cards. She didn't look much older than Maggie Scott and he guessed she wasn't the original wife but the trophy version. She was also evidently pregnant.

'No. It's Mrs McDonald.'

Maybe that explained a few things and Bracken wondered briefly if they had the right address, making a mental note to tear a strip off Sullivan if he'd put the wrong details into the satnav. 'Can we come in? It's urgent.'

She stepped aside and let the detectives in, then closed the big door behind them.

'We're looking for the family of Maggie Scott,' Bracken said.

'Honey, who is it?' a voice shouted from somewhere close by.

'Follow me, gentlemen.'

She walked across a tiled floor that probably cost more than Bracken earned in a year. A young boy, no more than ten, looked out past double doors that were open wide, his blonde hair all messed up. He smiled and ran to the woman, who Bracken assumed was his mother, but then he put that thought on hold. He'd already made a wrong assumption.

They went into a living room that was in proportion to the outside of the house. A large TV mounted on one wall showed a game of golf being played out. A man who looked to be in his late forties, owner of the aforementioned trophy wife, sat on a leather couch, apparently trying to decide whether he should pull himself away from the screen for a moment.

'These are the policemen I told you about.'

'Oh, come on,' he said, slapping his leg. 'I could have sunk that one with a cricket bat, for God's sake.' His attention span now broken, he turned to the detectives. 'What can I do for you?'

As he looked at them, Bracken recognised the man. Scottish justice minister Stuart McDonald. Natalie Hogan's ex-husband.

It had been years since he'd seen him, but despite the hair, which had receded more, and the crow's feet round the eyes, which seemed to have welcomed more family to stay, the features were basically the same.

'Mr McDonald, I'm afraid I have some bad news,' Bracken said, watching as the cogs in the man's head turned while he tried to place the big detective's face.

'Your name escapes me,' McDonald said, giving up.

'DCI Sean Bracken. DI Jim Sullivan.'

The judge clicked his fingers and stood up. 'Christ, how could I forget? The man who almost got fucked by Ailsa Connolly. In more ways than one.'

'It was an undercover operation, sir; we were never dating.' Bracken gritted his back teeth for a moment.

'Language, Stuart,' McDonald's wife chided, but if the boy noticed, he didn't say anything.

'Rory doesn't pay attention to me.'

Rory, the little boy Natalie Hogan had told Bracken about. Her son. McDonald had replaced her with a younger model and Bracken wondered briefly if the new member of the family due imminently had been Mrs McDonald's idea or the justice minister's.

'They're here about Maggie Scott,' the wife said. *Catriona, the husband-stealing bitch* as Natalie Hogan referred to her.

'Maggie? What has she done? She's not in trouble, is she?' McDonald asked.

Bracken looked at Rory, the handsome little boy who was unknowingly breaking his mother's heart.

'Could we have the wee fella go into another room?' he asked.

McDonald looked at his wife, expecting her to scoot along now, take the child and let the grown-ups do the talking, but Catriona was having none of it.

'Rory, go and play in the living room.'

'Okay.' He smiled at Bracken and ran off to another room. Bracken had thought this space was the living room, but apparently not. It was the size of an airport departure lounge, so God knows what this family thought of it as.

'What's the problem?' McDonald asked, and

Bracken thought at first he had read his mind about the size of the room.

'I have to ask you, are you related to Maggie Scott?'

'Maggie's our live-in nanny. What's wrong?' McDonald's face was a mixture of anger and panic, an expression that didn't appear too often.

'I'm sorry to tell you that she's dead.'

'Oh, Jesus,' Catriona said, one hand going to her mouth and the other to her swollen belly. 'How? How did it happen?'

Bracken hesitated for a moment. 'She was murdered. In a property that's currently up for sale on the outskirts of the city.'

'Fuck me,' McDonald said. 'When did it happen?'

'We're not sure of the time of death yet. She was only discovered a couple of hours ago. The details are still to be determined.' Bracken looked at the wife. 'When was the last time you saw her?'

Catriona took her hand away from her mouth and attempted to speak without falling apart. 'Oh dear God, please tell me this is a mistake.'

'Please sit down,' Sullivan said, and she did. 'How along far are you?' He nodded to her belly.

'Six months.'

'I know this is difficult, but we need to find out who killed Maggie.'

'I understand,' she said, trying to stay composed,

but tears started running down her cheeks. 'She was such a good girl. So good with Rory.'

'We saw her yesterday afternoon, right before dinner,' McDonald said. He too sat down and the two detectives followed suit, Sullivan taking out a notebook.

'What time, roughly?' Bracken asked. 'It's important we establish a timeline.'

McDonald nodded, his eyes seeing something else, a memory of the last time he'd seen the young woman. 'Around four-thirty, I think. It was before dinner.'

'She had the weekends off. From Friday evening until Monday morning. Yesterday was different,' Catriona said.

'How so?' Sullivan asked.

'She was going to see her boyfriend.'

'What boyfriend?' McDonald said. 'I didn't know she had a boyfriend.'

'Well, she did,' Catriona said. 'She told me and I asked her to keep quiet about it for the time being.'

'Why? Is he a prisoner or something?' McDonald ran a hand through what hair was remaining.

'No, of course not. Maggie wasn't stupid. He was married. Going through a difficult divorce. His wife would have made life hell for them. She confided in me that they were looking to get married after his divorce was final.'

'Were you going to let me in on this?' McDonald said.

'You've been busy with work. It was a women's thing. What would you have said to her if she'd told you that she was seeing a married man?'

'I would have told her she's stupid.'

'That's not what you told me when you were married to somebody else.' Catriona looked at her husband, but he didn't have an answer.

'Did he ever come round to the house, here?' Bracken asked.

Catriona shook her head. 'No, that wasn't something I was comfortable with. I told Maggie. She said she was fine with that.' She looked at them. 'Wait, you don't think this Peter guy had anything to do with her murder, do you?'

'It's something we're looking into,' Sullivan said.

'Of course they do, Cat,' said McDonald. 'That's why they're here asking questions about this mysterious stranger.'

'He's our main suspect, yes,' Sullivan confirmed, 'but we don't know much about him.'

'Does Maggie have any next of kin?' Bracken asked.

'No,' said Catriona. 'She doesn't have any family anymore. Her mother died last year, just before she moved in here with us.'

'Did she go out dancing or anything like that?' Sullivan asked.

'She lived here, but there's a separate entrance to her apartment round the side, so she could come and go as she pleased at the weekend. She assured us she didn't bring anybody home, but she got in late sometimes. An Uber would drop her off at the gate. She wasn't noisy and she was so easy to get on with. Rory is going to be devastated.'

'Was the white BMW hers?' Sullivan asked.

'It's ours, but she used it to take Rory to school and she could use it in her free time. It was as good as hers.'

'Does it have some tracker subscription service on it?' Bracken asked.

'Yes. The service with the stolen vehicle recovery.'

'Can you give BMW a call and tell them the car's been stolen?'

'Oh God. Yes. I'll go now.' Catriona got up and left the room.

Bracken looked at the justice minister for a moment. 'Mr McDonald, have you heard the name Andrea Harrison?'

McDonald thought for a second before shaking his head. 'I don't think so. It doesn't jump out at me. Why?'

'She was another victim. She was found yesterday morning.'

'Two in two days? Jesus.'

'It's unusual but not unheard of. Some killers go on a spree, then lie low for a while, recharging their batteries. I think those guys are the most dangerous. Sometimes there's no pattern, but this time the common denominator is this married man, Peter.'

'You think he killed them both?'

'It's something we're working on,' Bracken replied.

'Oh come on, Chief Inspector, stop shitting me now; is he your main suspect?'

'He is. We think he goes out with these women, telling them he's married so they won't talk about him too much to their friends, then he kills them.'

'Have you checked Maggie's phone?' McDonald said. 'Maybe she took a photo of him.'

'Forensics have it now. I don't think this killer would allow his photo to be taken. There's the possibility that she took a covert one, but I'm not holding my breath.'

Catriona walked back into the room. 'It takes just seconds to trace a car. They found it. Its location is a scrapyard near Ratho.'

Bracken and Sullivan stood up.

'Be very careful,' Bracken said. 'I don't think you have anything to worry about since you can't identify the killer, but use caution.'

McDonald didn't see them out, but his wife did.

She pulled the door to behind her, not closing it all the way but just enough to afford them some privacy.

'Can you keep a secret?' she asked the two detectives.

'Considering our job, that's a very tall order,' Bracken said.

Catriona took in a deep breath and let it out slowly. 'Okay then, but just don't let my husband know if you can help it. It's about Maggie. She had a little drinking problem. She shared it with me one night. This was before I hired her to look after Rory. I had known her for a while before I suggested she come to work for us full time. She was an alcoholic, but she'd kicked the habit. The thing is, she still went to see a psychologist to keep on the straight and narrow.'

'You know the doctor's name?' Sullivan asked.

'Robert Marshall, up at the Andrew Duncan Clinic.' She slipped back into the house like a ghost and the front door gently closed on them.

End of conversation.

EIGHTEEN

The car wasn't technically inside the scrap merchant's but rather parked in a little two-car parking area outside. Bracken stopped his car behind the patrol cars and the forensics van and he and Sullivan stepped out into the cold air once again.

Charlie Nelson and Izzie Khan had come along from the crime scene to meet Bracken and Sullivan.

'Funny place for a parking bay,' Bracken said.

'This is on a bus route, sir,' Nelson said, coming across to them. 'It's an infrequent service and comes through from Ratho, going up onto the main road and ending up at Wester Hailes centre. Sometimes people from the scrap centre will wait here, mostly during the week. Only one or two, but it's a busy wee route sometimes.'

'How are you such an expert on this?' Bracken said.

'A bus just came by a few minutes ago and I stopped it to talk to the driver.'

'And here's me thinking you were being clever. What about CCTV from the scrapyard?'

'They have cameras, but they only cover inside and as far as the little car park they have for employees. The trees there block the view of this part of the road. We just spoke to the manager of the place.'

'Nobody was outside and saw somebody park this and hop on a bus?'

'He didn't get on the bus. The driver I spoke to has been round here twice before this trip and he didn't pick anybody up.'

Bracken pulled up his collar against a cold wind that swept the snow around. 'How many of you have trampled your boots around the car?'

'None of us. We made sure not to step on the snow on the pavement. There are no footprints. And as you can see, a gritter truck has been round spreading salt, so the road is wet but clear.'

Bracken nodded and looked at Sullivan. 'Somebody picked him up or else he walked up the road. And it's a fair trek to the main road.'

'Maybe he walked up to the park 'n' ride,' Izzie said, walking across to join them.

Bracken looked at her. 'How far is it from here?'

'A good walk, the driver told us,' Nelson said. 'Like

134

when my parents used to walk to school, so they told me; it's all uphill, in the snow.'

'There are paths round here, though,' Izzie added. 'There's one that goes round the side of the technology building and it goes under the bypass into Edinburgh Park. Or there's another one further up the road that he could have taken. I looked at Google Earth and it goes along the side of the canal and continues on the side of the viaduct that crosses over the bypass.'

'Have a uniform nip up there and see if there are footsteps in the snow,' said Bracken. 'Doesn't mean anything if there are, but I want a clearer picture.'

'He must know his way around here,' Sullivan said. 'He feels comfortable. I don't think he left the car here by accident.'

Bracken looked at Nelson. 'Didn't I tell you two to go to the estate agent's office?'

'We hadn't left by the time you called us, boss. We were about to,' Nelson said.

'Right. Get going now then.'

'Yes, sir.'

He and Izzie got into their car and Bracken watched the Ford go over the small bridge ahead, the road narrowing down to one lane.

'The day's getting away from us now, Jimmy. We'll get back to the office and see what we have already. Is Angie there?'

'Yes, she is. I called her in this morning. She's putting things together on the whiteboard.'

'Let's go. We'll have to wait until forensics process the car. I don't think the McDonalds will be seeing it again any time soon.'

NINETEEN

Sullivan drove Bracken back to the station in his car, with Bracken suggesting that perhaps a primate might have better driving skills.

'I've taken an advanced driving course,' Sullivan retaliated.

'Whereabouts? At the fucking shows in Burntisland? The dodgems don't count, son.'

'It's harder to feel the brake pedal with boots on.'

'You'll feel my boot if you smack my head off the dashboard.'

'Might be beneficial if you put your seatbelt on,' Sullivan said as they neared Haymarket.

'Might be beneficial if you went home tonight and stuck a game on your son's Xbox,' Bracken said.

'You were in safe hands,' Sullivan replied as he parked the car in the small car park behind the station.

'If you call seeing your life flash before your eyes being in safe hands, then you and I have a very different outlook on life.'

Sullivan smiled as they went in the back door and up the stairs. Bracken didn't want to run up them, fearing a coronary might take him down before he'd had even half a chance to cut down on the Kit Kats.

DS Angie Paton was sitting on a chair in front of a computer, clacking away at the keyboard.

'Oh hello,' she said as the two men came in.

The old-fashioned radiators were kicking out plenty of heat and Bracken had no doubt he could quite easily put his feet up on one and doze off. Instead, he looked at the whiteboard.

'What do we have so far?' he asked.

Angie turned towards them. 'Both victims were young women. Not married, and now we know they had a boyfriend, somebody we're presuming was the same man, Peter Wallis. Nothing seems to connect them, or at least it didn't until I dug deeper.'

'Ailsa Connolly,' Bracken said as he and Sullivan took their coats off.

'Correct. Andrea Harrison was on the legal team who defended Connolly. And Maggie Scott worked for Justice Minister McDonald, who was instrumental in getting Ailsa Connolly moved to the new secure unit at the Royal Edinburgh.'

'On Monday morning, I want the father of Andrea Harrison interviewed again, just to see if he recalls something that might help us.'

'Yes, sir.'

'We also need to focus on where this Peter Wallis met them,' Sullivan said.

'We'll talk to the McDonalds again,' said Bracken, 'especially the wife, since it seems that Maggie confided in her the most. Maybe she'll remember some detail. Otherwise, we'll wait on forensics and the crime lab to come back and see if they have anything.'

They bounced ideas back and forth, then Nelson came in with Izzie.

'Well?' Bracken asked.

'There's only one other property like the other two, and it's a farm near Livingston,' Nelson said.

'Give the details to Angie and she can coordinate with uniform. Maybe have patrols swing by frequently on their way to the chippie or something.'

'Will do.'

Bracken sat down on a chair and wheeled it over to Angie's desk, taking his notebook out. 'Get hold of Ian Peffers, the property photographer that Edward Curtis told us about, and see if he's been to either the farm or the country house we were just at, taking photos. We ran them both through the system and they're both clean. Doesn't mean anything, though.'

'We spoke to him regarding Curtis's wallet and he confirmed that they did go looking for it but couldn't find it. He seems okay, very helpful.'

'Let's talk to him again.'

'We'll locate him and have another word,' Sullivan said.

Bracken looked at Angie. 'Did you make the call?'

'I did. He's expecting you.'

Bracken nodded his thanks and turned to the others. 'Right, folks, I just have one more thing to do and then we should call it a day. Finish up here, then Monday morning I want both families spoken to again. Izzie, you and Nelson can drive through to Fife to speak with Andrea's father. I want to go and speak to Catriona McDonald without her husband there. I'm assuming he'll be lording it down in the Parliament building.'

'Yes, sir,' Izzie replied.

Bracken got up out of the chair and grabbed his coat. 'For those of you who don't know, I'm going to visit Ailsa Connolly in the hospital tomorrow. It should be fun.'

'Like the last time, when she tried to kill you?' Nelson said with a grin.

'Only with her cooking, son.'

'Where are you going now?' Sullivan asked.

'To go see somebody.'

Bracken walked out of the incident room and thanked God it was all downstairs from here.

TWENTY

Morningside was crawling with traffic by the time Bracken got to the hospital. A sea of red lights lay in front of him, and he looked at the clock on the dashboard. He hoped the man would still be there; if he knew what was good for him, he'd better be.

Finally, he turned off the main road and into Morningside Park, then into Morningside Terrace, and he was at the old part of the Royal Edinburgh. He parked in front of a one-story building that might have looked like a country house somewhere if there had been mountains and trees behind it, but all he saw was a dowdy building in need of a lick of paint.

Snow covered the car park and he walked carefully to the entrance. His knee still gave him gyp sometimes. He had partially dislocated it years ago when he was drunk, an injury he hadn't felt at the time, but by the time the alcohol wore off, he couldn't move his leg.

Inside, it was evident that no expense had been spared on the heating bill. He loosened his overcoat and walked up to reception.

'I'm here to see Dr Marshall.' He showed the old woman his warrant card and she looked like it was something he had got out of a lucky bag. She pulled on reading glasses and made a face as she squinted at it.

'Hmm,' she said, as if still not fully convinced, but it was nearly knocking-off time for her, and as long as the big man standing before her wasn't holding a machine gun, it would be okay for him to go in.

'Through the door, turn right, third door on the left.'

She pressed a button and he heard a buzz and the door on his left clicked. He thanked her and grabbed the handle, pulling it.

Then he was in.

Turned right, found the third door on the left. The name plate on the door told him he was at his destination. He knocked and waited.

'Come!' a disembodied voice said from the other side. Bracken turned the handle and pushed and stepped into what could be the lion's den.

But this lion was a man heading for his fiftieth birthday, albeit with a good head of hair. Grey mostly, but still there, and Bracken knew some men would kill for such hair. He himself kept his hair short, but this man had no such aspirations.

One thing that grabbed Bracken's attention was Marshall's walking stick.

'Chief Inspector Bracken!' Robert Marshall said. This wasn't the defensive, arrogant prick Bracken had been expecting and it surprised him for a moment.

'Dr Marshall.'

'Oh, call me Robert. Everybody does, including the surly old woman on reception. She just gives the impression she's got a urinary tract infection, but she's harmless.' He smiled as Bracken shut the door and stepped further into the room.

There was a classic couch on one side, with a couple of chairs. An office chair sat tucked away into a small desk that had some folders on it.

'I'm glad you could come around,' Marshall said, holding out a hand. 'Your sergeant called and asked if it was okay, and I said I always have time for Scotland's finest.'

Bracken shook the doctor's hand, watching for any sudden movement from the other hand. None came.

'Coffee?' Marshall asked, indicating for Bracken to take one of the chairs.

'I'm fine, thanks.' He sat down and Marshall sat

opposite him, like they were in the classic doctor–patient mode.

'Ailsa has told me all about you, of course. The past you had with her.'

'It was undercover work. We were never dating.'

'Of course not. If you say so.'

'I do say so.' Bracken realised he was sounding defensive, while Marshall was sitting there smiling. The bastard was good; he was already inside Bracken's head, messing about with him. Bracken had a different way of messing with people, and it consisted mainly of Doc Marten boots and leather gloves.

'Are you here for good?'

'Can anybody ever say how long they'll stay in one place?' Bracken replied, making eye contact with the older man. Older, but not by much.

'That's the beauty of life, Sean. You don't mind if I call you Sean, do you? Good. Some of us are content to remain part of the pack, while others are natural hunter-gatherers. It's what I call the caveman syndrome.'

'I've met a lot of men in my time who closely resembled the missing link right enough.'

Marshall laughed. 'Ailsa would have so liked to have been here, but she's otherwise engaged. Does she know you're coming back to work in Edinburgh?'

'Not unless you've told her.'

'I haven't. I only found out myself a couple of hours ago when one of your detectives called me to arrange this interview. It is an interview, isn't it?'

Bracken hesitated for a moment. 'It's an informal meeting.'

'Still can't use my first name, Sean, can you? Please don't feel uncomfortable. It's better we stick to last names in a formal interview.'

Bracken smiled. 'You know this isn't a formal interview, or else I would be conducting it at the station. As I said, it's merely an informal chat we're having.'

'Like tomorrow's little informal chat with Ailsa?' Marshall's smile was almost a smirk, not quite smarmy but next door to it.

'That's right. I missed her annual call. We used to do Christmas cards, but now it's a phone call. Like me calling my aunt before Christmas and promising to go round and see her, but I never do.'

'Well, this "aunt"' – Marshall made air quotes – 'is looking forward to seeing you. She told me over lunch that you were coming around with a card this year.'

'Not a card but maybe a cake with a file in it.' Bracken looked away, at the diplomas on the wall. They looked like something you could download from the internet and print off. He turned back to Marshall. 'You can have lunch with Ailsa?'

'Of course. Every day. And dinner, if I don't have a

patient in. This isn't a death camp, Sean. The patients have rights. They just don't have the key to the door.'

'Must be hard, knowing your wife is within reach, yet tantalisingly just out of reach.'

'We manage. In fact, we have a good game of cards most evenings. But I'm sure you didn't just pop along here to pass the time, Chief Inspector.'

Bracken looked at the man to see if there was anything hidden in his words, but if there was, he couldn't see it.

'Peter Wallis,' he said simply, looking for a reaction.

Marshall smiled. 'I'm sorry, I'm not familiar with this game. Do we just throw names out at each other? What are the rules?'

'The rules are, when we catch this bastard, we're going to throw away the key.'

Marshall stopped smiling. 'In all seriousness, Sean, I haven't heard of that name. Two women have died and it's not something to be taken lightly. I heard on the news about a second victim.'

'You know how these people are just as well as I do. But this guy is different.'

'More of a spree killer than a serial killer.' Marshall was quiet before talking again. 'He took the eyes, didn't he?'

'How did you know that?'

'You forget what I do for a living. You came here

because you think I married Ailsa and therefore I'm somehow involved in the killings. Stands to reason, doesn't it? Maybe somehow if there are new victims it will throw doubt on Ailsa's conviction. I don't know how you came up with the name Peter Wallis, but in the back of your mind, you're thinking Peter Wallis doesn't exist and I'm in fact the killer you're looking for. How am I doing so far?'

'I'd be lying if I said you were on the wrong track,' Bracken answered, stealing a look at Marshall's walking stick.

'I'm not going to deny that Ailsa killed those men, because she did. She wasn't of sound mind back then, but she's come on leaps and bounds. However, I would stake my whole reputation on her being innocent of some of the accusations against her.'

'Like the kids.'

'Like the kids,' Marshall agreed.

'That's the sticking point, isn't it? The fact that kids were involved. Otherwise, the path to Ailsa getting released would be a lot smoother.'

'It's not a game we're playing, Sean. But cast your mind back to when she killed those men, each one deserving it: did you ever consider somebody else could have been involved?'

Bracken shifted in his seat. 'Of course we did.

Standard procedure unless we catch them standing over the cooling corpse holding a bloody knife.'

'I don't think you gave her innocence much thought.'

'Of course I did,' Bracken said, maybe a little too forcefully. 'I thought back to when I'd shared a drink with her, whether she said anything incriminating at the time, and I couldn't think of anything.'

'But you still nailed her for killing the men. Am I right in saying there was no physical evidence linking her to the murders of those children?'

'You know you're right, Doctor.'

'And Ailsa confessed to killing her six victims.'

'She did,' Bracken admitted.

'And not once did she ever admit to killing the children.'

Bracken drew in a deep breath and let it out. He knew Marshall was right, but he was finding it hard to admit that he had been wrong about Ailsa.

Marshall smiled at him. 'Without wanting to get on your bad side, I have to point out that the person who killed those kids did what Ailsa had done: he took their eyes. That was all. He copied the MO.'

'You keep saying *he*. How do you know it wasn't a woman who killed the kids?'

'We don't, but statistically it's more likely to be a

man. It all goes back to the dawn of time, when a woman was the protector of her young.' Marshall held up a hand. 'I'm not saying two men living together or married can't protect their young, but in a woman it's *instinct*, if you will. Something that's there that they don't have to think about. Ever seen Mama Bear charging at some- body who's touching her cub? That's why it's my opinion that a man killed those children, not Ailsa.'

Bracken didn't say anything for a moment. He agreed with Marshall. He hadn't agreed with the defence's argument back when Ailsa was on trial, but he agreed with them now. He stood up.

'Thank you for your time, Doctor.'

Marshall stood up and offered his hand again. 'Five years,' he said.

'I'm sorry?'

'I've been using a walking stick for five years. Back injury. I have terrible sciatica and they can't operate because of a heart condition. I couldn't fight my way through a wet newspaper, never mind tackle a young woman and kill her. But anything I can do to help, please don't hesitate.'

'Oh, there is one more thing. Maggie Scott. She was a patient of yours.'

'Yes, but I can't discuss her details with you.'

'I'm not asking you for any details. I'm just letting you know she was murdered. She's the second victim.'

Bracken left the office. He walked back out to his car feeling dejected. He'd hoped he would find the smoking gun, but Marshall was as likely to be the killer as Bracken was.

He got into the car and drove to what was to be his home for God knows how long.

TWENTY-ONE

Bracken found himself sitting in the living room again, having tucked into a superb dinner. Bob poked his head round the door and came in when he saw Bracken was alone.

'Hey, pal, how's it going?'

'Full tilt, Bob.'

'Of course it is, that's why you're sitting here watching TV instead of being out there catching a killer.'

Bracken looked at his friend for a minute to see if he had suddenly become unhinged. Then Bob broke into a smile.

'I remember those bastards saying that to us back in the day, as if we couldn't have any time off. How's it really going, though?' He sat down on a chair, on the edge, like a dog waiting for a ball to be thrown.

'There's a connection to Ailsa Connolly,' Bracken said, not sure how far he should go with divulging information.

'I fucking knew it!' Bob said, his eyes wide. 'She's connected there, Sean; I can feel it. That was too much of a coincidence. She's up to her neck in this. God, I hate that cow. I wish she would just roll over and die.'

'Take it easy there, friend. You don't want to end up having a stroke.'

'I know, pal, I know. That wouldn't do at all. Me in the hospital while that bitch is thumping her bible. I don't know what the church sees in her.' Bob looked towards the drinks cabinet. 'Fancy a wee yin?'

'I could murder a beer,' Bracken replied. 'I brought some more in. Tinnies this time. I can grab a couple if you like.'

'You sit there,' Bob replied, standing up.

At that moment, the lounge door opened again. Bracken saw annoyance cross his friend's face, but then Bob saw who it was and broke into a smile.

'Come away in, love. Sean and I were just about to have a tin or two. You fancy one?'

'Oh, listen, I know you two have a lot to catch up on,' said Natalie. 'I was just going to watch some boring TV. I won't disturb you.'

'Nonsense. You don't mind, do you, Sean?'

Bracken was painted into a corner by the two faces, so he just smiled and accepted his fate.

'Not at all. I'm the newcomer here. Don't let me spoil your routine.'

'You make me sound like Cinderella,' Natalie said, walking into the room. 'All work and no play.'

'Then you shall go to the ball. Or at least the living room.'

'And I don't have my glass slippers on, just my old, comfy flats.'

'I'm sure you'll be up in bed before you turn into a pumpkin.'

'As lines go, I've heard better,' Natalie said, smiling as she sat down.

'Bloody smooth-talker, this one,' Bob said, before departing the room. Hopefully to another dimension, Bracken thought, not knowing if he could survive an onslaught of innuendos by the Chuckle Brothers. But no, his friend was back in record time with three tinnies, and he dished them out before sitting back down.

Natalie was about to put the TV on when Bracken caught her attention.

'I want to tell you this because the news will be all over it shortly, and it's better coming from me first,' he began.

'Look, Sean, what you do in the privacy of your

own room...' Bob started to say, but shut up when he saw the look on Bracken's face. 'Sorry, pal.'

'I was called to a murder scene today. A young woman, just like yesterday.' Bracken looked at Natalie, giving her his full attention. 'It was Maggie Scott.'

Natalie looked confused as she cracked her tin with one hand, pulling the tab back and forward like she could do it in her sleep.

'Who?'

Not the answer Bracken was expecting. Then he asked himself, *What* were *you expecting, Sean? Tears? A look of horror on her face, just before she jumped up, telling you she had to go and comfort her ex-husband?*

Yes.

'She was Rory's live-in nanny. His...' He was about to say 'mother', but caught himself in time. '... step-mother was going to have a talk with him.'

'His what?' Natalie said.

'Poor wee guy,' Bob said.

Natalie looked puzzled as she took a sip of the lager. 'I didn't know he had a nanny. Don't you think Stuart should have told me about that? Rory is still my son, after all.'

'He should have. The bastard. I'll call him up and give him my tuppence worth,' Bob said.

Christ, Bob had been watching period dramas

again. Tuppence was two pence in new money, something like that.

'Let's just stay calm here, Bob,' Bracken said. 'Whether or not he asked anybody's permission to hire a nanny, let's not forget she's dead. Murdered in a brutal way.'

'That was a hell of a quick turnaround for Rory,' Bob said, sitting back in the chair. 'He'll be upset.'

'And Catriona has to look after herself in her condition,' Bracken said.

'What condition?' Natalie asked.

Bracken looked at her and took a drink from his can, buying himself a precious couple of seconds in order to ensure his next words came out like a bunch of roses, not hollow-point bullets.

'She's pregnant.' Christ, he never was any good with the roses.

Natalie's mouth opened a couple of times like she was trying to form words, like somebody dying at the side of the road with only seconds to live.

'Pregnant?' she said eventually, her voice soft.

'Six months,' he said, not meaning to rub salt in the wound, but there was no denying the salt was there.

'I wonder why he didn't tell me.' She looked at Bracken. 'Stuart, I mean. Or Rory.'

'They probably had the wee boy schooled, telling him not to mention it,' Bob said.

'That's why Stuart always came round on his own with Rory. Ready to jump in if my son started to say anything out of place.'

For a moment Natalie looked like she was going to cry, but then she composed herself and took a drink of beer.

Bob followed suit, knocking some back and Bracken could see uncle and niece sitting drinking into the wee hours, systematically slagging off Natalie's ex. So much for Bracken and Bob chewin' the fat over the old days.

'I'm in the mood for getting blootered,' Bob said. 'What say you, Sean?'

'I'd like nothing better, my friend, but I'm going to meet Sarah.' The lie came easily as Bracken looked at his watch. 'Going to have a quick shower first. Don't let me stop you, though.'

'We've got plenty of time to have a wee sesh, Sean. Christmas coming up and all.'

'Aye. Cheers.' He drank some more and put the can down on the table. 'I'll catch you later, Natalie,' he said, not wanting to mention Maggie Scott again. He got the feeling his mentioning the dead woman's name wouldn't be appreciated.

He shaved and showered, figuring shaving now would save him doing it in the morning, and showering out of habit in an attempt to wash the stink of death and decay off himself – but no matter how much he scrubbed, he felt the death of the others still lingering on him.

He went back downstairs, debating whether to stick his head into the lounge. Hearing angry voices coming from in there, he stalled, listening. He was about to move on when he saw the old couple watching him.

'Mr and Mrs Clark. How are you this evening?' He smiled at them, feeling like they'd just caught him kneeling down at a keyhole. The small hallway was lit by a little lamp on a table and Bracken hoped his face wasn't going red.

'We're fine, Inspector, thank you,' Mrs Clark said.

'Been doing a little Christmas shopping for...you know...' Mr Clark nodded in the vague direction of the back of the house.

Christ, Bracken would have to remember to do some Christmas shopping of his own.

'I'll end up doing mine at the last minute, no doubt,' Bracken explained. 'I was wondering where you were at dinner.'

'We're too late and I'm starving,' Mrs Clark said. 'Never mind, it'll soon be breakfast time.'

Bracken's heart sank; he felt sorry for the old couple. He only had his old man now, whom he didn't get to see that often, but at least Bracken looked after him. He took his wallet out, took out some money and held it out to Mr Clark.

'Here. Order a chippie or something. Have it delivered. It's not too late. You shouldn't get heartburn if you order it now.' Words he had said to his dad many a time after the old man complained about eating too late. Heartburn or farting, or sometimes both. Bracken had heard all the stories about how old folks' guts couldn't handle eating late, but it didn't stop the old bugger trying.

'Naw, son, you're alright. Appreciate it, though,' Mr Clark said, and Bracken could see the disappointment on Mrs Clark's face. Bracken looked at the bags; it was hardly Louis Vuitton they had been shopping in.

'I insist. Honestly. You missed a good meal. Mary does a really good dinner, as you already know, so I'm not hungry. But you too look like you could do with a wee fish supper to yourselves. Here, that should cover the food and the delivery and a tip for the driver.' He reached forward and put the money in the old woman's hand.

'Thank you, son,' she said, squeezing his hand. 'You're a good boy.'

He smiled as he walked out into the cold.

Down at the bus stop, he only had to wait ten minutes. He wiped some of the condensation off the inside of the window as he sat upstairs, the bus filling up rapidly as young people headed into town. Drinking, dancing, puking in the back of a taxi for some, getting lucky for others – and some of those catching something nasty they'd have to talk to a doctor about.

Bracken thought about Catherine, his ex-wife. He wondered if she was seeing somebody. He'd spoken to her on the phone just a week ago, but neither had brought up the subject of the other one's sex life. Bracken's was non-existent.

He got off in Princes Street and walked up the North Bridge. A blast of wind nearly took his woollen hat off and snow was coming down again. He looked at his watch; quarter past eight. *Shit.*

He took out his phone as he stepped it up a notch and hit a speed-dial button.

'Cameron? How you doing, son?' Cameron Robb, his old DI back in Fife.

'Not so bad, sir. How's the Wild West?'

'Same as it ever was. But listen, pal, I have a wee favour to ask, if you don't mind.'

'Sure. Fire away.'

Bracken told him what he wanted.

'I'll get right on it first thing Monday morning.'

'Good lad. I owe you one.' He ended the call after promising he'd go back to Glenrothes one night for a good old piss-up.

He stepped up the pace and waited to cross at the

traffic lights. Then he was inside the Inn on the Mile. He looked around briefly, trying to spot the familiar face, but couldn't find it. He ordered a pint and looked around again, more slowly this time. Still nothing.

He paid for his pint and stood at the bar like Norrie Nae Mates. One pint, then he would just get the bus back home.

Another exciting Saturday night under his belt.

TWENTY-TWO

'You look like you're contemplating going to a singles' club,' a voice said from behind him.

He turned around. 'That obvious?' he said to Chaz, who was standing there smiling at him.

'Sad, desperate, lonely. And that's just the barman.'

He smiled. 'I didn't see you.'

'That's because I'd left. I was outside and happened to look over and saw you walking in. You like to keep a woman waiting, don't you?'

He looked at the snow on her hair, wet in places, and on the shoulders of her long overcoat.

'The bus was heaving,' he said.

'Sure it was.'

'Where's everybody else?'

'Oh, they couldn't make it,' she said with a cheeky smile.

'Couldn't make it or weren't invited?' he asked.

'You choose whatever answer you want to believe.'

He wondered if he should make an excuse and leave, but he didn't. 'What you having?'

'Pint of lager, thanks.'

'Of course. I wouldn't expect anything else.'

'I hope that was meant as a compliment, Sean Bracken.'

'It was.' He looked down at her Doc Marten boots. Trousers, not a dress or a skirt. Somehow, although he hadn't known her long, he couldn't picture this young woman in a dress.

He ordered another pint and a couple rose from a table. They sat down.

'Cheers,' Chaz said.

'Here's to us,' Bracken said, and saw Chaz's eyebrows raise as he took a sip of his lager. 'Oh, no, I meant –' he started to say.

'Rabbie Burns,' she said, laughing at his embarrassment. 'You haven't been around a woman in a long time, have you?'

'I do alright. In fact, I was in the company of a woman last night.'

The smile slipped a little bit and he could see in her eyes she was wondering if she'd made a mistake inviting him along here, even for a friendly drink.

'I was in the guest house and it was another guest. I only just met her.'

'Hey, it wouldn't matter to me. I only asked if you wanted a drink to welcome you to the fold.' She drank some more.

'Exactly. Does your husband know you're out gallivanting with other men?'

'I'm not married.'

'You have a slight discoloration on your wedding finger. I just thought maybe you had taken it off to come out for a drink.'

'*Was* married. Not anymore. My husband thought it was more fun to go out shagging around with other women than to stay at home when I was called out after hours.'

'Sorry.'

'Don't be. He's remarried, lives down south with his new hoor, I mean wife, and I haven't seen him in two years.'

He squinted his eyes slightly at her. 'How old are you?' he asked.

'Don't say it like you think you've picked up a fifteen-year-old schoolie.'

He laughed. 'Just curious. You look so young.'

'That might have had more of an impact if I was fifty, but I'm thirty-two.'

He looked her in the eyes to see if she was joking.

'Seriously? You don't look a day over thirty-one.'

'Come on, Bracken, you don't have to try so hard with the compliments. I'm only out for a drink with you. We would have to meet up at least three times before you could put a ring on my finger.'

'Is that what the three-date rule means?'

'Yeah, something like that.'

'How come you didn't ask me if I'm married?' he asked her.

'I have a unique talent. Here, let me show you. Give me your hand.'

He held on to his pint like she would steal it if he put it down. She had already put hers on the table.

'Come on, give me your hand. The dry one, not the wet one holding the glass. Although you might want to put the glass down or else you might drop it in shock when you see my hidden talent.'

'Hidden *and* unique. I expect my socks to be blown off.' He gave her his left hand and she took it, closing her eyes for a second.

'You were married once,' she said.

'That was easy. I have a daughter. Fifty-fifty chance I was married to her mother.'

'Wait a minute,' Chaz said, looking at his face. 'I'm not finished yet. Her name is...Catherine. You've been divorced for...going on six years now. You moved to Fife to work with the force over there before deciding to come back here. You don't have your own place yet.'

'I just told you I was talking to one of the other guests in the guest house. But how did you know my ex's name is Catherine?'

She let his hand go. 'I told you, I was once part of a duet called Hidden and Unique. We had some talent.'

'Just as well you weren't called Free and Easy,' he said.

'Are you calling me free?'

'Yeah, that's what I was going for.'

She laughed. 'Cheeky sod, Bracken.'

'Tell me, how do you know my ex-wife's name?'

'Okay, you've worn me down, copper. Please back off and I'll tell you anything you want.' She leaned in closer. 'Bob Long is always coming around the mortuary. He tells us everything that's going on in his life. Including you coming to stay. And about how you all used to go out as couples.'

'Why are you whispering?'

She sat up straight. 'Sorry. Didn't realise I was.' She took another drink. 'So there you have it. You beat it out of me.'

'Don't be saying that too loud, for God's sake. People might hear you and think it's true.'

She laughed. 'Just when you thought I was special, you get the truth from me.'

'I *do* think you're special.'

'I walked into that one.'

'Do you have a boyfriend?' he asked her.

'They're beating a path to my door, didn't you notice?' She shook her head. 'No, boyfriend-free at the moment. I'm on the desert island of dating, with no hope of rescue on the horizon. What about you?'

'Nope. No boyfriend.'

'Don't make me ask.'

'No girlfriend either.' He held up a hand. 'I know, I know. Hard to believe, isn't it? Young guy like me, single and available, with no dame on my arm.'

'Dame?' she said. 'Who talks like that?'

'I was binge-watching *Downton Abbey*.'

'I hardly think they refer to women on there as *dames*.'

'You know what I meant. I might have heard my dad say it now and again.'

Then Bracken wondered why he had come along here tonight. Making new friends? No, he didn't need any new friends. Desiring the company of a woman? That was never a bad thing, but he could have stayed in the guest house and listened to Natalie talk about the new book she had planned, *101 Ways to Kill Your Ex-husband*.

'You want another one?' Chaz said.

'Only if you tell me what Chaz is short for.'

She hesitated. 'Charlene. What's Sean short for?' She walked away to the bar before he could reply with a smart-arse answer.

'It's Seamus, if you must know,' he replied when she sat back down with the drinks.

'Have a feel of the back of my head. Are there buttons there?' Chaz smiled and clinked her glass with his.

He started to feel more comfortable as they idly chatted about work. It was good conversation with a colleague, nothing more.

'Do you live around here?' he asked her.

Chaz waved a hand in front of her face, feigning shock. 'Why, I do believe the gentleman is overstepping the boundaries.'

'I was going to say I would wait at the bus stop until your bus came along.'

She looked at her watch. 'Jeez, ten thirty. You in a hurry to get home or something? What happens if you're not in by twelve? Bob and Mary won't let you out to play again?'

'I'm an old man, remember? Not a wee schoolie like you.'

'Forty-five is hardly old,' she said.

Bracken just looked at her, silently asking her how she knew how old he was.

'Bob Long really needs to get out more. I'm

surprised he didn't tell Pam your shoe size.'

'He was talking to Pam and you just happened to be earwigging?'

'I was in the room and I don't have cloth ears.'

He drank some more and smiled at her. 'I like the way you can dodge a question and steer the conversation away from the original question. Maybe I should be worried. Maybe you're an ex-con who's been through the mill. Like you know the drill.'

'Yeah, that's the image I was trying to convey when I asked you along here tonight.'

He got a couple more drinks in, then his phone rang. Cameron Robb. 'Sorry, I have to take this,' he said, getting up from the table, and he walked over to where the toilets were.

'Cameron, m'man. How're things?'

'I got you that info you wanted, boss.'

'I thought you were going to wait until Monday?'

'I figured that it would be more private this way.'

'Good man. Let me get my pen and my wee pad.' Bracken fished the items out of his pocket and stood to one side. 'Shoot.'

Robb gave him the information. 'Thanks, pal. I'll be coming through soon and we'll have a few. On me.'

'I look forward to it, boss.'

He used the facilities and went back to the table. Chaz was gone. He stood and grabbed his glass, finishing the dregs, then prepared to leave. He didn't know if he felt disappointment or not. It was only a drink with a friend, after all. *A friend now?* he asked himself. *She was a colleague a wee while ago.*

Ah, fuck it, he thought and was about to walk away when he felt a hand on his arm.

'I thought you were going to walk me to the bus stop?' Chaz said, smiling at him.

'I thought you'd left.'

'I wouldn't leave without saying goodbye. I was using the wee girl's room.'

'Fair do's. What bus you getting?'

'Same one as you. I live just off Station Road in Corstorphine. And we can even sit upstairs and sneak a fly puff on a ciggie. Since I'm only a schoolie.'

A man at the bar turned round to look at Bracken.

'She's only kidding,' he said. 'See?'

The man looked at Chaz, then turned back to the bar.

'Come on, let's go, before you get me into a fight,' Bracken said.

'I don't really smoke, by the way.'

'I don't care one way or the other.'

'Yes, you do.'

'Whatever. You win. Now let's just go.'

They took the bus into Corstorphine and got off at the stop before Station Road.

'You could have got off at the last stop,' Chaz said to him.

'This is just as easy. You want me to walk you to the end of your street?'

'Sure. Let's walk and I can hold on to your arm. If I go down, we go down.'

'You're hardly wearing stilettos.'

'True. I'm not a high heels sort of lady, but when I go out on a date, I don't always wear boots.'

Bracken found this hard to believe.

They chatted some more and turned into Station Road. Just down on the left was her street, The Paddockholm.

'My flat is just over there.' For the first time that night, she looked awkward. 'I would invite you in, but...'

'Goodnight, Chaz,' he said, smiling at her.

'Goodnight, Seamus.' She laughed as she walked away.

The two figures sat in the dark of the car with the engine running, watching the young woman interact with the older man.

'I thought he would have gone inside with her,' the first one said.

'Doesn't matter. It doesn't change things. She'll never know we were there.'

They both watched until the woman walked into the communal stairway of the small block of flats, then they drove away.

TWENTY-THREE

The Sunday church crowd were out in force as Bracken drove along Colinton Road. The roads were wet with melted snow, with the promise of getting covered that night. He dodged an old woman in a car as he listened to a man on the radio who was cheerier than anybody had a right to be. Maybe he was secretly drinking. It was the perfect job to have a drink problem.

He was sweating in the car, his brow slick. Maybe it was the thought of coming face to face with the woman who would have killed him that night had he not been on the ball.

Technically, he would have been Ailsa Connolly's seventh victim. Some people would have argued the numbers, saying she killed five children too, but she was never charged with their murders.

The last time he had seen her was a year after the start of her sentence. He had gone with her to the farm in Fife, where they had discovered the badly decomposed remains of her last victim.

He took a left along Myreside past the Watsonian Club and another left into the new Royal Edinburgh hospital.

He shook his head in disbelief. He still found it hard to understand why Ailsa Connolly was now classed as a medium-security prisoner. She had been moved into this building three years previously when it had opened, having been transferred from Carstairs State Hospital.

The doctors had listed the reasons for the move as good behaviour, passing psychiatric evaluations and God knows what else. The move had been approved by the Scottish justice minister, and the contractors had made a secure unit with a wing that only housed Ailsa. Nobody was quite prepared to throw all their eggs at one time.

He parked his car and walked along to the main entrance. The wind spat snow at him until he walked into the warmth of the building. He introduced himself to the young woman sitting behind the desk at reception.

'If you wouldn't mind waiting here, please,' she said. 'The clinical director will meet you.'

Bracken sat down, unbuttoning his coat. There were magazines on a side table, some with curled edges and a look that suggested they might be harbouring some form of plague.

The building was warm. As it was only a few years old, it was draught-proof and kept at a decent temperature. Unlike his old station. Christmas decorations were strung from the ceiling, and a Christmas tree sat in a corner, with bright lights and ornaments. It reminded him that he hadn't started his Christmas shopping yet and to get a move on.

It was just another thing he'd had to deal with since the divorce, but it amazed him that he had to mentally kick himself up the arse every year. He and his ex-wife still exchanged cards, and this year's card had the words, *Remember Sarah's Christmas card!* He had forgotten last year's, and the big box of chocolates he'd given his daughter still hadn't made Catherine happy.

'You are the detective, yes?' a man said, approaching. Bracken stood up quickly, thinking that this was somebody who had escaped from a ward.

'Dr Fritz Meyer.' The man smiled and held out a hand.

'DCI Sean Bracken. Major Investigation Team, Edinburgh West.'

The doctor's handshake was strong and firm, as if

he worked out with one of those little spring hand exercisers. The rest of him apparently didn't take part. He looked about the same age as Bracken, but with a pot belly and a chin that was well on the way to being a double. He let go of Bracken's hand.

Meyer was dressed like an old-fashioned professor, like he belonged in another century, with a brown tweed jacket and a bow tie. Bracken waited a moment to see if it was one of the spinning ones he'd seen in a joke shop, but it wasn't.

'I'd like to speak with Ailsa Connolly,' he said. 'She's expecting me and all the arrangements have been made.'

If Meyer's smile didn't exactly fall off a cliff, then it was certainly hanging on by its fingertips.

'Before you go, I would like to warn you that Ailsa isn't the same woman you arrested six, seven years ago.'

'In what way?' Unless it was the fact that her hobby was making sculptures out of wood with a chainsaw, Bracken didn't see any reason he couldn't visit her.

'She's been getting better and better every day. Advancing towards her degree. Seeing you might set her back. I want to throw that out there.'

'Duly noted, but don't you think that if she were on the outside, something might just as easily trigger one of her unhappy moods? Or do you see her popping some pills before you let her go?'

Meyer looked puzzled. 'Who said anything about letting her go?'

'If one day she does get deemed fit for release, I mean.' There was a headache bouncing a ball in Bracken's head, and he knew that it would only take one little blow of the ref's whistle for it to start a full-blown game. This little man with the funny name and the funny clothes was rubbing him up the wrong way, like an itchy woollen sweater against bare skin.

'Look, Dr Meyer, things have been arranged and I really need to talk to her.'

The smile was gone now, all pretence of liking the detective put back in the jar and the lid screwed down. 'Very well. I wanted it on the record in case it goes tits-up. The orderly will take you up.' Meyer swept an arm for Bracken to follow and his line of sight took in the white-suited man with the shaved head standing off to one side, waiting. All he needed was some homemade prison tats and he was set.

'Come on then, Twinkle Toes, take me to her.'

Meyer exchanged looks with the orderly, as if they were going to toss a coin to see who would smack Bracken first. He hoped it would be the big man. He didn't fancy ripping Meyer's bow tie off and making him cry.

They rode the lift in silence and went through

several locked doors before they got to the small secure wing Ailsa Connolly had to herself.

She was sitting in a chair in what looked like a living room at first, until Bracken looked closely and saw the lack of anything that could be deemed a weapon.

The orderly stood off to one side, and Bracken wondered if the fat bastard could move, if push came to shove.

'You're looking good, Sean,' she said, smiling at him.

'You too. Married life is agreeing with you, I see.' And it was. Ailsa had lost a fair bit of weight, but she didn't look skinny, just like a woman who looked after herself. Her hair had flecks of grey in it, but he suspected they allowed her to use hair dye.

'Robert and I are very happy. Sorry I couldn't send you an invitation, but things were hectic enough. Still, you're here now.'

'I missed your phone call the other day. Now I know why: you cast me aside for another man.'

'You had your chance way back when.'

'I think about that all the time.' It wasn't exactly a lie; he had thought about it almost every night for a long time afterwards. The beautiful woman who he suspected wanted to sleep with him, yet who was equally happy stabbing him. Or worse.

'Did they tell you about me studying to be a minister? Wait, of course they did. They told you everything there is to know. About Robert.' She paused for a moment. 'He told me you spoke to him yesterday.'

She looked at him, studying his face as if she was trying to catch him out in a lie, waiting for him to deny he had spoken to her husband.

'He's a very likeable man.'

'He took over the role of force psychologist for Edinburgh and the surrounding areas.' Spoken like she had read it off a pamphlet.

'I didn't know that.'

'Of course you didn't. Big, bad Sean Bracken doesn't need to go and speak to somebody. Big tough guy.' She moved in her seat and Bracken jolted ever so slightly, but she did nothing more dangerous than change her position.

'How long do you have to go before you become a fully fledged minister?'

'A while yet. I have to be with a minister for fifteen months after graduating, then I get my own church.'

She said it like she was going to be out any day soon. He looked into her blue eyes, glinting with life, and tried to read her. Was she playing with him? She was a psychologist after all. Playing with people's heads was her game.

'How's Sarah?' Ailsa asked him before he could

speak again. There was a slight smile on her face, not quite cocky, but letting him know she still remembered everything there was to know about him.

'She's fine.'

'Robert had a daughter. Did he tell you that?'

Bracken shook his head. 'No, we didn't get as far as swapping family photos.'

'She was murdered. By some thug. He was just bad, through and through. Nothing could change him. Robert's daughter had the misfortune of getting off at the same bus stop as him. She was stabbed to death, but nobody witnessed the killing. Nobody actually saw him commit the crime. He was a suspect, nothing more. Now he's walking the streets.'

'I'm sorry to hear that.' And he was. It was never easy to hear about somebody's child dying. It was even harder when you had to investigate their murder.

'Look after Sarah, Sean. She's the most precious thing in your life.'

He thought it was a threat at first, but realised it wasn't. 'I know she is.'

'You would do anything to protect her, wouldn't you?'

'Where's this going?' he asked, starting to feel irritated.

'You came here, remember?'

'I wanted to ask you about Peter Wallis.'

She paused for a second. 'Who?'

'Do you know Peter Wallis?'

'The name doesn't ring a bell.'

'What about Andrea Harrison and Maggie Scott? They ring any bells?'

Ailsa shook her head. Then smiled. 'Catriona McDonald does, though.'

'Catriona? You know her?'

'Yes, I do. She was a patient of Robert's when he still did the alcoholic counselling. She wasn't married to McDonald at the time, and she needed help with some issues. Robert wanted her to come and see me, because he felt she was hesitant in opening up to him. She didn't want to come. Something was holding her back.'

'Somebody killed her nanny, and another woman. He's working fast and he's leaving them like you left your victims: without eyes. I think it's somebody you know, whether you realise it or not.'

'And you want me to help you?'

'I'm asking you to help stop more killings. Innocent young women are dying.'

'Now you want my help?' The smile was gone from Ailsa's face.

Bracken felt the heat seep into him more now.

'You denied killing those children back then,' he

said. 'I was on the fence about it, but now I can see how quickly you can change.'

'You can believe what you want, Sean. I didn't kill those children.'

'You're the only one who believes that, but it's not me you have to convince, is it? It's the justice minister. He's the one who'll be able to release you on licence if he deems you're mentally fit now.'

'I've come a long way since then, and I don't want to go back to that place.'

Bracken searched her face. He thought he knew how to read people, but he had never been able to read Ailsa, not entirely.

'Again, not me you have to convince.'

This seemed to stir something inside Ailsa, a little bit of passion. 'Not everybody holds a grudge like you, Sean. Billy Burton's moved on. He goes to see Robert. I don't have to tell you about how your friend and colleague Bob Long tried to save Burton's grandchildren and broke his back falling through the burning floor. Burton held on to the anger for the longest time, but now he's healed. He just needs to talk to Robert regularly, and since Robert is the force's psychologist, that's acceptable.'

'I don't think it's acceptable that Robert discusses his patients with you. What if Burton found out?'

Ailsa smiled again, enjoying the verbal sparring.

'Robert doesn't discuss all of his patients with me. Billy Burton is of special interest to me because he thought I'd murdered his grandchildren. I didn't. It got to me that he thought I did, and Robert was merely reassuring me that Burton doesn't hold the anger towards me that he once did. Bob Long too.'

'I think a lot of people hold anger towards you.'

'I wouldn't know. I only know that Burton still sees Robert.'

'Did you know that Burton's son killed himself? Took an overdose.'

Ailsa looked puzzled. 'No, I didn't know that. That's a shock. Poor guy. I knew he'd moved away from the area. I didn't know he had killed himself.'

'Losing your wife and kids has that effect on some people.' He stood up. 'You know a lot of people question why Jesus lay dead for three days, but they forget that his spirit was out and about.'

'What makes you say that?'

'You're in here, but your spirit is out there killing. You might not think you know the killer, but I'm willing to bet he's crossed your path at some time.' He nodded to the orderly. 'Give me a call if you can remember who he is.'

Ailsa stood up but maintained her distance. 'I'm sorry, Sean. This will be the last time you see me. I've moved on now. No more phone calls, not even our annual one. I have my husband to think of now.'

'Try to think of innocent women being murdered. Their lives could be in your hands.'

He turned and walked out of the room with the orderly.

He didn't look back.

TWENTY-FOUR

Bracken was about to go upstairs when Mary came out of the residents' lounge with a cloth and a can of furniture polish in her hands.

'Oh hi, Mary. How's Bob doing? I didn't see him at breakfast.'

'Truth be told, he was a bit rough this morning. I had Natalie help me before she went to work. He's away out for some fresh air, he said.'

'I know he wants me to sit with him, and I will, but –'

'But nothing, Sean. You have your own life. He has plenty of time to chat with you. I know it must be boring for you, but he doesn't have many friends just now. They all cut him loose after he broke his back.'

'It's not boring. I don't mind. I just had to talk to

Sarah last night.' It wasn't exactly a lie, and he genuinely wouldn't mind sitting with Bob, but he would prefer it if it was just the two of them. 'Maybe we'll go to the pub one night.'

'He'd like that. Sometimes he forgets he's not on the force anymore.'

'I know, Mary, and I want to talk shop with him, but there are some things I just can't talk about. I *do* feel bad, but I would rather feel bad than compromise a case.'

'I understand, love.'

'If it's easier for me to go, I can find somewhere else.'

'Are you kidding me? You will not leave, Sean Bracken. I love having you here. It makes me miss the old days, our nights out, the laughs we had, but I also realise that time marches on to its own beat. We can't turn back the clock, and the sooner Bob realises that, the better. I mean, I'd love to be twenty-one again, but that's not going to happen.'

'You look just fine the way you are.'

'Always were a smooth-talker, eh, Mr Bracken.' She smiled at him.

'I can try.'

'Oh, before I go, I have this for you.' She reached into her jeans pocket and took out a slip of paper and handed it over to him. 'I think she likes you.'

He took it and read it: *I should have given you my phone number last night. Just in case you want to share a bus again sometime. Chaz.* Her phone number was next to her name.

'She came here looking for you a little while ago. She seems nice,' Mary said.

'She's somebody I work with. Well, she's at the mortuary.'

'You don't need to explain. But if I were you, I'd call her. Before somebody else does.'

She turned to walk through to the back of the house. Bracken stopped her.

'Is Natalie here? I wanted to apologise for rushing out last night. I think she was settling in to watch a movie and I feel like she misses having company around. I bailed on her and Bob.'

'No, she's working. I wouldn't worry about it.' She walked away again.

Bracken went outside, got into his car and dialled the number, keeping the fan speed low, just enough to keep him warm.

'Yes, I'm happy with my electricity provider, no, I don't want a warranty for my car and I already give to charity,' said the voice on the other end.

'It's me, Seamus,' he said, but then the voice started again.

'Anybody else can leave a message after the tone.'

Christ, who makes a recording like that? he thought as he heard the beep. He wasn't sure what to say at first.

'You're either a lousy heavy-breather or you're lost for words,' Chaz said.

He was still silent, not sure if it was really her or not.

'Hello. You've reached the voicemail of Seamus McSeamus. Leave a message.'

She laughed. *'Seamus McSeamus? Now I really do know you're daft.'*

'Daft enough to listen to your recording all the way instead of hanging up.'

'Now you've got my full attention, do you fancy grabbing a coffee?'

'Where's open around here on a Sunday?'

'Tesco has a little café.'

'Pick you up in a couple of minutes?'

'I'll be waiting.'

He drove around the corner and into Chaz's street. She came out a couple of minutes later, wearing light-blue jeans this time but still the boots.

'Still couldn't find your stilettos, eh?' he said as she put her seatbelt on.

'I think I'm going to need to find them soon just so I don't look like a little person standing next to you.'

Bracken put the car in gear and wondered briefly just what the hell he was doing. He had known this woman for five minutes, but he'd come running after she left her phone number for him. Was he desperate?

The answer was, yes. Maybe that was why he had sat and listened to Natalie the other night. She was female company, no matter how flawed she was. Now here was another woman wanting to be in his company, even if it was going for coffee at Tesco. He knew he shouldn't knock it.

They chatted while he drove along and parked as far away from the door of the supermarket as was humanly possible.

'Will I call us a taxi to get us to the front door?' Chaz said with a smile.

'I refuse to park anywhere close to these Neanderthals. You see the way some of them push a trolley around the store? Then they come out and get behind the wheel of a car. Some cars have a "baby on board" sign in the back window and sometimes I think the baby must be driving.'

Chaz giggled. 'Relax. I'm just pulling your chain, Sean. It's fine. I know how men like their cars.'

'I just hate it when somebody scrapes another car and then they bugger off.' He smiled. 'I must sound like a real old fart moaning about his car.'

'Maybe next time we'll take the bus.'

Inside, it was warm after their trek from the car across the frozen tundra. They went up the travelator to the upper level, got their coffee from the Costa there and sat down.

'Do you come here often?' Bracken said, then closed his eyes, shaking his head.

'Dearie me, Sean. You need to brush up a wee bit.' She laughed. 'But to answer your question, no, I don't come to the coffee shop often. I shop here, though. Not very romantic, is it?'

Is that what this is? he thought. *Something romantic?* He was still at the 'having a coffee with a friend' stage.

'Oh, I don't know. You can have a drink, there're lots of people around and they play music. I've been on worse...' He was going to say 'dates', but stopped short. This was not a date. Chaz was a friend, nothing more.

It made him think of a friend of his who had taken offence at Bracken divorcing his wife. For some reason, he'd seen the breakup of Bracken's marriage as their friendship breaking up.

'You know something, Bracken?' the man had said when they were in the pub one night. 'You're nothing but a fucking scumbag.'

If anybody else had said that to him, Bracken

would have clocked the bastard, but he just drank up and left the pub.

His friend had apologised the next day, but that had been the beginning of the end and shortly afterwards his so-called friend stopped calling.

The few friends Bracken had left behind when he had moved to Fife were nowhere to be seen now. Only Bob Long had stayed in touch.

'Yeah, I've been on worse too,' Chaz said, grinning.

'Tell me about yourself, Chaz,' he said to her.

'There's not much to tell. I'm divorced, as I told you last night, and I live on my own – no kids, no pets. I have a house plant that's still alive, but I don't hold out much hope for his long-term survival. I don't have much luck with plants.'

'Gotcha. No kids, no husband, plant killer.'

'When you put it like that, it makes me sound like a real sad case.'

'Until you listen to my profile,' Bracken said. 'Divorced, grown-up daughter, lives in his friend's guest house, no girlfriend, no pets, no plants.'

'That profile screams, *Marry me! I'm desperate.*'

'If that was on one of those dating sites, you would swipe right past. I make hunchback look like a good catch.'

'I do see the resemblance to Quasimodo, mind.'

'If you think I'm doing an impression of Charles Laughton, then you can think again.'

She laughed and picked up her bag. 'Just going to the little ladies' room.'

Bracken was looking over at the display cabinet, wondering if he should boost his blood sugar level, when he saw Natalie over by the men's clothes.

'Hi, Natalie,' he said, putting a hand on her shoulder. But it wasn't Natalie. 'Oh, sorry. I thought you were somebody I know.'

'Natalie McDonald?'

'Yes. Is she around?' Bracken thought if he could have a quick word, then he could apologise for giving her the brush-off last night.

'I know her. She called in sick this morning.'

'Oh, okay.' He sat back down at the table. Called in sick? But Mary had said Natalie was away to work. Strange.

'What do you normally do on a Sunday afternoon?' Chaz asked as she sat back down.

'Recover from Saturday night. What about you?'

'Nothing exciting. Sometimes I go out with friends. Other times I just catch up with some films. Give my plant CPR if he needs it.'

She was talking away, but Bracken's mind drifted. Why would Natalie call in sick and lie about it? There had to be an explanation.

Then his phone rang. He took it out of his pocket and looked at the screen, thinking it was his daughter, but it was Jimmy Sullivan.

Just then, Chaz's phone rang. She looked at him.

'I think we're about to have our Sunday ripped apart,' she said.

TWENTY-FIVE

Natalie McDonald wasn't sick, she was spying. That's what they would say after they arrested her.

Before that happened, she was standing on the other side of her ex-husband's garden wall, looking through some bushes to see if she could catch a glimpse of her son.

She was being gripped by the cold despite having her hoody pulled up. This served as double duty since this neighbourhood was security conscious and more than one property had cameras.

She knew the courts wouldn't take too kindly to her doing this, but at the end of the day, it was a public street and she wasn't doing anything illegal.

She looked over the wall and saw that Stuart's Mercedes SUV was gone. Typical of him to go golfing on a Sunday, even in the bitter cold. She suspected that he didn't even make it onto the greens but only got as far as the bar. He didn't have far to drive home.

Natalie stepped back from the wall. Too late, she saw a car approaching. The driver, an elderly woman, didn't honk the horn but waited until Natalie was out of the way. Still, Natalie jumped in shock and, forgetting all about keeping her face away from the road, she looked directly at the woman before stepping out of the way. She smiled weakly and raised a hand in an apology, and the woman made a face as she drove past.

This only stoked the fire inside Natalie. Stuart was supposed to bring Rory round for a visit yesterday but had called at the last minute to cancel, saying their son had been invited to a party and so they would just see her on Christmas Eve as planned.

Not even Christmas fucking Day.

She was here to try to plead her case with Catriona. She seemed to be the sensible one.

Natalie walked down the narrow road onto the main road and turned into the driveway. The gate had been left open and she walked up the snow-covered driveway.

One final look back towards the gate and then she walked up to the door and rang the bell.

A few minutes later, Catriona McDonald

answered. 'Natalie? What are you doing here? Is Stuart expecting you?'

'No. It's you I've come to see. Can I come in? I won't be long.'

Catriona hesitated for a moment, then stepped back to let Natalie in.

TWENTY-SIX

They decided it would be quicker and easier to share a car to go to the crime scene. Chaz could grab a white suit from Pamela Green's car, as the pathologist always carried spares.

'We're almost the same size,' she said as Bracken put his foot down, heading over Drum Brae. This wasn't going to take long at all.

'How long have you worked at the mortuary?' he said, honking his horn at a bus pulling out and navigating round it. He turned onto Queensferry Road.

'Two years. And I'd like to be there for a little while longer, if you don't mind.'

'Don't worry, you're in safe hands.'

'Said the captain of the *Titanic*.'

Five minutes later, they were pulling up to the big house in Barnton. In the drive were patrol cars, an ambulance and a couple of unmarked cars, including Pamela Green's. Bracken had to stop just outside the entrance. He showed his warrant card to the uniform guarding the scene.

'I wonder who lives here?' Chaz said, impressed.

'The justice minister, Stuart McDonald.'

'How do you know that?'

'I've been here already.'

Inside, the heat was fighting the cold coming in through the constantly opening front door. Bracken put on overshoes while Chaz took a white suit from Pamela.

The scene of crime team were wandering around taking photos, having already photographed the victim.

Catriona McDonald was lying in a pool of blood on the couch, the blood spreading out from underneath her in a crimson lake, soaking into the flowery fabric. There were multiple stab wounds and her throat had been cut. But one standout feature drew Bracken's attention.

Her eyes had been taken.

Suited up, Chaz knelt beside Pam, helping her to lift the body to look underneath.

Pam slipped her mask up. 'She's not been dead that long. Less than an hour.'

Just then, DI Jimmy Sullivan walked in. 'I've just been coordinating a door-to-door, but it isn't going to be easy. The street is full of high walls and high hedges. Unless somebody caught something on a camera.'

'Keep trying. Have you located the husband yet?'

'No. We're still working on that.'

'Where's the little boy, Rory?' Bracken asked. His heart was beating faster now.

'We can't find him. He's nowhere to be found in the house.'

'Well, get it searched again. Get more bloody uniforms in here and search every space, including the attic if they have one. Everywhere. I want to know he's not hiding, scared out of his wits, before we hit the red button on this one. Go now, Jimmy.'

'Yes, sir.'

Sullivan left the room, and a few minutes later he came back in with a group of uniforms and instructed them to pull the house apart.

Bracken took his phone out and called Mary at the guest house.

'*Hello, Sean,*' she said.

'Mary, is Natalie there?'

'*She is. She said she wasn't feeling well and went right up to her room. Do you want to speak to her?*'

'No, that's fine. I won't disturb her. But let me ask you: did she come in alone?'

'*Yes, of course. What's this about? You're starting to worry me.*'

'I'll tell you later, Mary. I can't over the phone. Talk to you soon.'

He hung up and waited for Sullivan to come back downstairs.

'He's not anywhere to be seen,' Sullivan said when he eventually returned.

A uniform walked in and came straight up to Bracken. 'We've located the husband, sir. A neighbour said he plays golf along the road at the Royal Burgess. He's on his way back now, with a patrol escorting him.'

'Good job.' Bracken looked at Sullivan and indicated for him to step aside with him.

'You know McDonald's ex-wife lives in the guest house where I'm staying?'

Sullivan nodded.

'Well, she was supposed to be working today, but I found out she called in sick.'

'Okay.'

'I want to know where she was.'

'You think she came here?'

'Possibly. I'm not ruling anything out,' Bracken said.

Just then, a man came rushing into the hallway of the house. 'Catriona!' he said as a uniform held him back. Bracken walked towards Stuart McDonald as he struggled against the uniform.

'My wife! Where is she? They said there'd been an incident at the house. Where's Rory?'

'Listen, Stuart, I want you to come with me through to the kitchen.' He held on to McDonald's arm and guided him through to the kitchen, followed by Sullivan.

'Sit down. We need to talk.'

McDonald was taking deep breaths as they sat at a dining table in the huge room.

'I'm sorry to tell you that your wife is dead,' Bracken said, knowing there was no time to beat about the bush.

'Oh my God! How can that be? I've only been away about an hour or so! What happened?' McDonald was about to get up, but Sullivan stood next to him.

'She was murdered,' Bracken told him. It looks like she was murdered by the same man who killed Maggie.'

'Oh fuck. He's targeting me, isn't he?'

'Could be, but we don't know for sure. Did Rory go anywhere before you left? Was he going to a party or something?'

'Oh God, no. He was here. He's not going anywhere. Where the hell is he?' There were tears running down McDonald's cheeks now, and Bracken had interviewed enough killers to know that either McDonald was a brilliant actor or he was innocent.

'We're trying to locate him now.'

'The cameras,' McDonald said just as Bracken was about to ask about Natalie.

'You have cameras here?'

'Yes. The footage is in the cloud.'

'Can you access it?'

McDonald wiped an arm across his face. 'Yes. I can do it on my iPad. It should be here. I was surfing the web at breakfast.'

He looked around and saw it. He got up and picked it up from the counter and opened it. The screen kicked into life and McDonald's fingers flew over it. He logged in to the camera app and the live view from the doorbell camera showed the vehicles outside. He scrolled backwards and it was like watching a movie in reverse. He went back past when the first patrol car arrived.

'We had a call from a neighbour about a stranger lurking about; that's when they sent the car out to check it out. The uniform saw Mrs McDonald lying on the couch and called it in,' Sullivan explained as McDonald kept scrolling backwards.

He went back in a blur, the picture losing clarity as it rewound, but then they saw Natalie walking up and ringing the doorbell.

'Oh God, no. Don't tell me she killed Catriona and took our son.'

They watched the video play out, but nothing happened and Bracken got McDonald to move it forward. Then Natalie came back out. She turned to look back at the house.

'Thank you, Catriona,' she said, her voice sounding tinny.

'Don't worry, it will be fine,' they heard Catriona reply.

'Bye, Mum,' Rory shouted and then the door was shut. Then Natalie walked down the driveway and out of sight.

'Catriona was alive when she left,' McDonald said.

'That doesn't mean she didn't come round the back,' Sullivan said.

McDonald looked at him. 'We have a camera there too. I can easily check.'

Just as he was about to check the recording from the back garden camera, Bracken saw a figure on the screen.

'Keep playing it,' Bracken said.

They watched as a hooded figure walked up the driveway, somebody bigger than Natalie and wearing a different-coloured hoody. Black, not grey like hers.

This figure kept his head down and made sure he didn't look at the camera as he knocked on the door.

They could see the back of his hood, and when the door was opened, he held something up for Catriona to look at. Then she let him in.

'Maybe Natalie swapped hoodies and came back,' McDonald said. Although he didn't really believe it.

'This guy is too big. Bulkier.'

'Maybe she had somebody working with her. She came here, killed my wife and took our boy. It's happened before.'

'We don't want to jump to conclusions and go off on a tangent,' Sullivan said.

They watched as ten minutes passed and the figure came out, this time holding Rory's hand. The boy was bundled up in a thick jacket and holding a teddy bear.

'Oh fuck, he took my boy.' McDonald looked at Bracken. 'Do you think he's working with Natalie?'

'I'm going to find out.'

Bracken left the kitchen and told Chaz what was going on.

'I'll see she gets home okay,' Pam said.

'Thanks.' Bracken called to Sullivan, 'Jimmy. With me. You think Angie can handle things here?'

'She can.'

'Right, you and me to the guest house.'

Bracken gave Chaz his best half-smile and she nodded back at him. Then he walked out the door.

TWENTY-SEVEN

Natalie was sitting in the living room watching an old black-and-white movie when Bracken got there with Sullivan. A patrol car was waiting outside as backup.

'Hey, how're things?' she said as Bracken walked into the room but then looked puzzled when Sullivan walked in too.

'We need to talk, Natalie.'

Her cheeks went red as she muted the TV and sat forward. Bracken kept his distance and both men watched her carefully.

'I didn't think we knew each other that well that we would be breaking up so soon.'

Again with the humour. Bracken knew it was a defence mechanism.

'We know you were at Catriona's house,' he said.

'Did she tell you that? Well, she was fine with it. I

just wanted a little chat about seeing Rory on Christmas Day and she said she would talk to Stuart. I hope she didn't just say that to get rid of me and then call you to complain.'

'Catriona's dead.'

'What?' She jumped up out of the settee and Sullivan braced himself. 'What happened? I was just there!'

'She was murdered, Natalie.'

She sucked in a breath like she was trying to suck all of the air out of the room. 'Oh Christ. Is Rory okay?'

Bracken didn't answer her at first, which made her step towards him and grab his arms. 'Is my boy alright?'

He moved his arms so he was grabbing hers now, but gently. 'Catriona was murdered in the same way as the others. He took Rory with him when he left.'

She collapsed. Again, Bracken thought that if she was acting then she was bloody good. Maybe she and her ex-husband had gone to the same acting classes. She sobbed and screamed and Mary came running through.

'Sean! What's happening?'

Sullivan stood in her way.

'She's family,' Bracken said to him, then turned to the older woman. 'Catriona's dead and Rory was taken by the killer.'

Mary's mouth opened and closed again, her breath coming in a whoosh of air.

'Where's Bob? Is he home yet?' Bracken asked.

Mary shook her head.

He turned back to Natalie, knowing time was of the essence now. 'I need to ask you this: do you know anybody who would take Rory away?'

'No! No, I don't know who would want to hurt my baby. Maybe you should ask Stuart!'

'Trust me, we're working on it.'

He left the house, leaving Mary and the uniforms to look after Natalie, and got Sullivan to make the call, getting everybody to the station.

When they got to the West End, it was all hands on deck. A manhunt had been launched, with the media involved. Uniforms were posted at the guest house and at McDonald's house. Especially the Barnton house, where the media were arriving in droves.

'The sightings are starting to come in,' Charlie Nelson said. 'Some people are calling in saying they've seen Elvis and Michael Jackson. Nothing of any use.'

Bracken nodded. 'Keep at it. Anything at all, get people onto it. We need to track every decent lead we get. How are we on CCTV?'

'There are a lot of vehicles going through Barnton at that time, sir,' Izzie said. 'Nothing stands out.'

'If only he'd been driving a clown car. Keep at it.

Get teams round the doors again. Talk to people who might have been out first time round.'

His stomach growled and he looked at his watch. Christ, it was going on seven o'clock. The past few hours had flown by.

He was walking down to the canteen to grab a cup of coffee when he decided to make a call. After being transferred and talking to somebody, the person he was after came on the line.

'My, my, twice in one day. You really are persistent, Sean,' Ailsa Connolly said.

'I was at a loose end and the only alternative was playing solitaire on my computer.'

'Still don't have a social life. I'm surprised. You need a woman in your life.'

'Not if they're all like you.'

There was silence for a moment before she answered, and he kicked himself. Not a great way to start things off, by insulting her.

'I heard about the wee boy and his mother,' she said. 'I'm assuming that's why you called.'

'Bad news travels fast,' he replied, not really in the mood to play games.

'Why don't you tell me why you called?'

He hesitated for a moment. 'I still need your help. I think you may know the killer without realising it.'

'Here we go, round and round. I already told you, I can't think of anybody who fits the bill.'

'What about Robert? You told me Catriona was one of his patients.'

'You'd have to ask him.'

'I already did, Ailsa. I keep hitting a brick wall.'

'Let me ask you a question, Sean: why should I help you, when you're the one responsible for putting me in here?'

'The night you tried to kill me, I let you live. I could have killed you in self-defence and nobody would have batted an eyelid. The headline would have been, *Hero Copper Kills Child Killer*. They would have pinned a medal on me.'

'Then why didn't you when you had the opportunity?'

'Because, Ailsa, I'm built differently to you. I wouldn't be able to sleep at night if I knowingly killed somebody.'

He hung the phone up and got the coffee from the machine.

TWENTY-EIGHT

Upstairs, more detectives were coming into the incident room, drafted in from other stations.

They worked the case hard, until finally it was time to go home.

'I won't be able to sleep,' Angie said. 'Knowing that wee boy is out there, and we don't know if he's dead or alive.'

'None of us will,' said Bracken. 'But if we don't get some kip, we won't be fit to do anything, and he'll need us to be giving it our all. So we need to come back fresh. The CID team will be here all night covering for us. Back in eight o'clock tomorrow, folks. See you then.'

It was gone ten now, and he was starting to feel hungry, but food would just sit in his stomach and give him indigestion.

As he drove along Corstorphine, he decided to risk

a chippie. A piece of fish wouldn't be too greasy, he told himself. On the fat bastard scale of one to ten, it surely had to be no more than halfway.

He was driving past Western Corner, coming up on the zoo, when he decided to call Chaz. He didn't have any reasonable explanation for doing so, but he hoped she would answer before he got to Station Road.

The phone rang and rang without an answer. *Fuck.* Maybe she was in bed already. It had been a long day for all of them.

The traffic was light at this time of night. No stinking bus crawling along to impede his travel, no taxi stopped wherever the hell it felt like.

He indicated and pulled over at the side of the road just after the zoo and before the guest house. He tried the number again.

'*Hello?*' a voice answered on the other end. It was a man's voice.

'Sorry, I think I have the wrong number.'

'*Yeah, no problem.*' He hung up and Bracken sat with his phone in his hand, knowing he hadn't called the wrong number. Obviously, Chaz had her boyfriend round.

'Oh well, Bracken, as you told yourself, it was coffee with a colleague.' He put his phone in his coat pocket and was about to drive away when it rang. He couldn't ignore it, thinking it might be the station.

He looked at the media screen and saw it wasn't the station. It was Chaz. Calling to apologise for leading him on? To tell him some sort of bald-faced lie, like the neighbour had popped over for a bowl of sugar and just happened to pick up her phone.

Now he understood why she didn't want him going up to her flat. Not that he would have pounced on her, but he didn't feel comfortable. Different if they were seeing each other as more than friends, then yes, just try to stop him, but fuck that, going up for a cup of coffee and idly chatting about the books she had on her shelf or what shows she watched.

The phone stopped ringing.

'God Almighty, Bracken, what are you like? You should have talked to her, listened to what she had to say, then if all wasn't well on the Western Front, you always had the option of telling her to go fu–'

The phone rang again. This time he hit the little telephone button on the steering wheel.

'Hello?'

'Bracken, was that you going to ignore me again? I know you knew it was me,' Chaz said.

'I'm sorry, you're breaking up.'

'No, I'm not. Silly sausage. Who did you think it was when you heard the man's voice on my phone? My ten o'clock appointment? Quick back rub and a hand

job? Or did you think it was the husband I didn't tell you about? Maybe my secret boyfriend?'

'All of the above.' His face was going red and he wondered if people on the outside of his car thought it was a mobile brothel with a red light inside.

'It's Roger, my brother. He just popped round for a coffee. God knows why he answered my phone. I've told him before not to do that. Anyway, he was just on his way out.'

'That's good. But I was just calling to ask you if Pam had started the post-mortem on Catriona McDonald. Sorry to be calling so late.'

'First of all, no, you're not, and second, no, you're not. You were calling because you had an ulterior motive, until you heard Roger's voice, and now you have to make up some shit to cover yourself.'

God, how did some women do that?

'Jesus, who needs a lie detector when we have you. Plug you in and off you go.'

'I'll take that as a compliment.'

'Right. I was passing, going to the chippie, and I was calling to see if you've eaten, but seeing what an ungodly hour it is, that was stupid of me.'

'Just a wee poke of chips, please. And I'll have the kettle on. You saw what stairs I live in. Top flat, on the right. And no jokes about giving me a poke.'

'One poke coming right up. Be there in ten.'

He hung up and drove along to the Bar B Que chippie. Foot traffic was light and he was in and out in a few minutes. Five minutes later he was parked and climbing the stairs to Chaz's flat.

There was no sign of Roger as Bracken went into the kitchen.

'My brother is an arse at times. He's very protective of me, especially since the divorce.'

'There's nothing for him to worry about since we're just colleagues.'

'That's what I told him.' She took the little tray of chips and they sat down in the living room at a little table off to one side.

'He's not hiding in the wardrobe, is he?'

'Or anywhere else for that matter. You're quite safe. But seeing as you're so big, I don't think you would have anything to worry about. Roger wasn't gifted in the height department. He's a little taller than me and I'm five-five.'

'Again, just colleagues sharing a chippie.'

'Sounds a lot better than you coming up here to give me a poke. I don't think Roger would have seen the funny side of that.'

'Let's not tell him then.' Bracken tucked into the fish and offered Chaz a bit of it.

'Jeez, Bracken, I'm trying to watch my figure.'

'You've nothing to be concerned about. Here, have a piece. Break it off yourself.'

He could smell some sort of perfume coming off her as she leaned in close to break a piece off. She had probably showered and he could smell the body wash. Jesus, it had been a long time since he had been this close to a woman.

She smiled and moved back with a piece of fish on her plate now. 'I'll need to cycle an extra couple of miles on my bike just to burn off those extra calories.'

'You cycle?'

'Stationary. I can go out in all weathers and still watch Netflix while I'm doing it.'

There were some photos in frames in front of books on a bookcase. He didn't ask if the books were read or for show, but there was an assortment of crime novels and thrillers.

'That's Roger there,' she said, nodding to the bookcase when she saw him looking. Chaz was standing next to a small man who was thin and balding. It made Bracken feel better about himself.

'He live close by?'

'Gorgie. He pops in now and again and we meet up for coffee. We've become closer ever since my mum and dad died in the crash.'

'Oh God, I'm sorry to hear that.'

'It was a couple of years ago. Just after I got divorced. Everything seemed to happen at once.'

'I've only got my dad these days. My mum passed away from cancer a few years back.'

They were silent for a few moments, then Chaz smiled. 'Well, now that we killed the conversation, would you like some more coffee?'

'Best not. I'll be up all night and we're going to be in the office early tomorrow.' He ate more fish and swallowed it with the coffee, which was only lukewarm now. 'Did Pam get you home okay?'

'Yes. She's really great. We started around the same time. Kindred spirits starting a new job.'

'Where did you work before?'

'For the NHS. In a lab. I saw this job advertised and decided to go for it. I loved my old job but couldn't stand the office politics. My boss acted like a demented old circus monkey. She was awful. We all ran the office while she skived off.' She ate a piece of the fish. 'You know, I was thinking about the case.'

'Me too. Poor Natalie. She's out of her mind with worry. So would I be if somebody had abducted my child.'

'No, I mean I was thinking about it. The whole reason those women have been murdered. The single thing that connects them. Where did he meet them?'

'We're still working on that.'

'If he's killing in the same way that Ailsa did, then why? Just like six years ago: he was copying her then, but I don't think he was just trying to copy her, if that makes sense. He was trying to get her into more trouble, as it were. It worked up to a point, but if she didn't get convicted on all charges, then he failed. There has to be a reason he's doing it again, while she's still in the hospital.'

'It's what we look at, motive.'

'And have you come up with one so far?' Chaz asked.

'Not yet.'

'Areas I would look at are where he met his victims and how the killings would affect Ailsa. One thing's clear.'

'What's that?' Bracken asked.

'He hates her. I mean, the last time he killed, it was to get her into prison, and that was achieved, whether he was instrumental in it or not. This time? This time it's personal. He hates her and he's doing it to get to her. Find the connection between his victims and that will connect you to him.'

'We're working on that too. There doesn't seem to be an obvious connection between the first two victims.'

They finished their food and Chaz took the wrappers away and came back to sit beside him.

'Let me ask you something,' Bracken said.

'Fire away.'

'Why did you ask me to come along for a drink last night?'

'I thought you might be needing a friend. Simple as that. Why did you call me and ask if I'd eaten tonight?'

'Because I thought you needed a brother, but you already have one. My job here is done.' He smiled and stood up. 'I'd better go. Up early and all that.'

'Me too. Thanks for supper. Best poke I've had in ages.'

Bracken groaned. 'Do you ever give up?'

'Not until I get what I want. Goodnight, Sean Bracken.'

TWENTY-NINE

While it wasn't exactly chaos at breakfast, there was an atmosphere. The uniform crew that had been present when Bracken had come home last night had been replaced by two more uniforms. Bob Long was talking to them when Bracken came downstairs.

'Excuse me, son,' he said to one of the uniforms. 'I'll make sure Mary gets you some breakfast.' He walked away and followed Bracken into the dining room.

'How's Natalie?' Bracken asked.

'Oh, you know, could be better. She woke up this morning and her son is still missing.' He curled his lip.

'We're doing everything we can –'

Bob put a hand up. 'Save it, son. I was in your shoes not so long ago, remember? I know all the trigger words.'

'Aye, sorry, Bob, I really am, and we'll do every-thing we can to get this bastard.'

'Maybe if you wired that bitch up to the mains, then she would tell you what happened and who took young Rory.'

Bracken could feel the hatred coming from every pore. But then Bob stopped talking as Mr and Mrs Clark came in.

'Good morning, folks,' Bracken said with a smile.

'Oh, good morning, Sean,' Mrs Clark said, smiling at him. 'That fish supper was rare last night.'

'Aye, it was that, son. Thanks again. I won't forget it,' Mr Clark said.

'Anytime.' Bracken poured himself a coffee from the catering flask and some cereal, but he wasn't too hungry. He forced himself to eat, not knowing when he was next going to get a meal.

Bob didn't join him, but Mary put on a brave front.

'If Bob seems on edge, please forgive him,' she said to Bracken. 'He was out drinking with Billy Burton yesterday. He just needs to get out sometimes.'

'Nothing to forgive. Natalie's family and we're all concerned. I'll take him for a beer one night.'

'He'd love that.' She leaned in a bit. 'Bob would hang Ailsa Connolly if he could. He hates her that much.'

'I always leave that sort of thing up to the courts.'

She patted him on the shoulder. 'Scottish breakfast?'

'No, thanks. Quick coffee, then I'm off.'

'Alright. If you change your mind, just holler.' She walked away to talk to the old couple, who were sitting at their own table now.

Afterwards, Bracken went to his room and thought about the text he had been sent last night.

Not stalking you, I promise. Just wanted to say thanks again for the...chips. Lol. Followed by a smiley face.

He sent a text back. *Anytime.* Smiley face.

For some reason, this young woman enjoyed being in his company. He wasn't going to knock it.

He opened up the phone app, looked at a recent number and called it, waiting for the other end to be picked up.

'Mr Harrison? It's DCI Sean Bracken. I need to ask you a personal question about your daughter, and please answer me truthfully. Was she in therapy for whatever reason?'

'She was. Not therapy exactly, but she went to an alcoholics' group meeting.'

'You don't happen to know who the therapist was, do you?'

'I do indeed. I picked her up one time and I met him. What a great guy. His name's Robert Marshall.'

Bracken sat still for a moment. 'Thank you. That must have been hard, but you've been a great help.'

'Just get the bastard who killed my daughter.'

Bracken hung up and hit the contact for Jimmy Sullivan. 'Jimmy. Find an address for Dr Robert Marshall, Ailsa Connolly's new husband.'

'I'll get right on it.'

Bracken grabbed his coat, pulled it on and buttoned it as he rushed down the stairs and out to his car. It was snowing again, but the remote starter had taken care of the ice on the windscreen.

On the way into the West End, Sullivan called him back.

'It's in Morningside, just round from the hospital.'

'Get over there now. I'll meet you there.'

Sullivan read the address out loud and Bracken had to think of how to get to it. He turned into Balgreen Road, knowing he was heading in the right compass direction. He pressed the voice control button on the steering wheel, and after three attempts at asking for directions and getting what sounded like two recipes and a quick lesson in how to speak Russian, he pulled the car over and typed the address in.

Then he realised it was around the corner from the hospital and he knew which way to go. The Monday traffic was a lot heavier than it had been the day before, but he made good time.

Jimmy Sullivan was waiting at his car, sitting with Charlie Nelson, and next to it was a patrol car.

'The door's wide open. We haven't gone in yet. Should we get a warrant?'

'The old boy might be in trouble. Let's just get inside.'

Sullivan turned to the patrol car and nodded to the two officers who were sitting in it, and they all went up the small driveway, which was taken up by a snow-covered Volkswagen Beetle. It sat in front of the door to a garage that didn't look big enough to fit the Beetle.

Just as Sullivan had said, the front door to the house was wide open. Time for the extendable batons. Bracken led the way, half-hoping that somebody would come charging out at him so he could vent some frustration.

There were what looked like several sets of footprints in the snow. Bracken moved into the house quickly, scanning the hallway and the doors leading off it. They were all open and not a sound was coming from anywhere, except the ticking of radiators fighting the cold that was rushing in through the front door.

'Check upstairs,' he said to Nelson and the uniforms, then he turned to Sullivan. 'Something's happened to him. He's not a fighter.'

Sullivan nodded. Then he pointed to something in the empty living room. Bracken looked. Marshall's walking stick. Bracken walked forward and that's when he saw the blood on the carpet. Not a lot of it, but a little drop, like maybe from a burst nose that somebody might have given Marshall if he had put up what little fight he could.

'Upstairs is empty,' Nelson said when they came back down. 'None of the beds have been slept in.'

'Right, Jimmy, call it in,' said Bracken. 'I think whoever took Rory also took Marshall, for whatever reason.'

'I wonder why?' Nelson said.

'I'm going to find out. I'm going round the corner to talk to Ailsa again. Meantime get uniforms to flood this area. Get them knocking on doors. Keep me in the loop.'

Sullivan nodded and Bracken left the relative warmth of the house and stepped into the snow, which was starting to come down harder. He got in his car, drove round to the Royal Edinburgh and parked in front of the secure unit.

Inside, a different woman was sitting behind the front desk. She at least had a smile for him as he showed his warrant card.

'I need to see Ailsa Connolly.'

'My, she *is* a popular lady today.'

'I'm sorry?'

'She already has a visitor. I'll see if she can see you afterwards.'

'She'll see me right away. I'd put money on it. Tell her it's about Robert.'

The woman's smile faltered as she picked up the handset and spoke into it in a low whisper, like she was making a prank call.

'Go right up,' she said after hanging up and she buzzed him through.

An orderly was waiting at the door to escort him. When they reached Ailsa's unit, a man in a suit was waiting outside. He put a hand up.

'You can't go in there.'

'That hand touches me, son, and you'll never wipe your fucking arse with it again. My name's Bracken. Remember it.'

The suit stepped in front of the door. 'In case you're hard of hearing, I'll repeat myself,' he said, poking a finger into Bracken's chest.

Bracken grabbed it and bent it back, but not all the way to breaking point. The man squealed and went down on one knee. An orderly opened the door.

Bracken let the man's finger go. 'You won't be picking your nose for a wee while, but you'll be okay eventually.'

'Fuck you,' came the reply.

Then Stuart McDonald was standing in the doorway. 'Bracken. Come in. And you,' he said to the suit, who still had one knee on the floor. 'Put in for a transfer. Useless bastard.'

'To be fair, I have had quite a bit of caffeine this morning,' Bracken said, stepping into the unit and listening as the door was secured behind him. He was shown into the living room.

'My, this is a nice surprise,' Ailsa said. 'The justice minister and a policeman all in one day.'

'For God's sake, Ailsa, do you have to be so flippant?' McDonald said, starting to pace.

'Okay, have you found Rory?' she asked.

'You know we haven't,' Bracken replied.

'And what's this about Robert? He refusing to play your games again?' She smiled at him, all cocky and brave, just like he remembered.

'He's gone.'

The smile dropped. 'What do you mean?'

'I mean, somebody has abducted your husband. There's blood in his living room and his walking stick is there too. His front door was wide open and there's no sign of him. Unless he decided to go for a walk in the snow without his walking stick and left the front door open on purpose, I'd say somebody took him. And I'm guessing it was the same person who took Rory.'

Ailsa sat down on the couch and for the first time

Bracken saw somebody who was utterly lost. Then she looked at him. 'Are you sure?'

'I'm positive.'

'We need to find them,' McDonald said. 'If you know anything, Ailsa, please tell us.'

'Robert lied to you, Sean. He thought you were going to try to involve him in the murders, so he kept something to himself.'

'What is it?' Bracken said, and the two men sat down.

'He did know Andrea Harrison.'

'I found that out this morning.'

'He also knew Maggie Scott. She met Catriona in group therapy.'

'Wait, what?' McDonald said. 'What group therapy?'

'Your wife and your nanny were both alcoholics,' Ailsa said.

'What? That's shite! I don't believe it.'

'Believe it, Stuart,' she replied in a soft voice. 'It's why she offered Maggie a job.'

McDonald rubbed his face and made eye contact with Ailsa. 'It's time you told Bracken.'

'Tell me what?' Bracken said, staring at him.

'It's about Peter Wallis,' Ailsa said. 'I know who he is.'

THIRTY

It was amazing how your day could turn to shit in the blink of an eye, Chaz thought, trying to stay calm. One minute there you were, getting ready for bed, the next there was somebody at the door.

She had felt excited when she heard the knock, thinking it was Bracken coming back because he had forgotten something. Jesus, she hadn't felt this way about a man in a long time, and she understood they were just friends, but after a long drought of male company, this man coming into her life was a Godsend.

She pulled the front door of her flat open and smiled, but then the smile dropped and a scream choked in her throat as the man wearing a hoody and ski mask punched her on the nose.

She felt her legs giving out and she overbalanced as pain shot through her face and blood started pouring out all over her fucking carpet. She landed heavily on her backside, and all the things she'd been taught by Roger, all the videos she'd watched on YouTube about self-defence went out the window. The man reached down and grabbed her hair, making her stand up pretty quickly, and he slammed the door behind him.

If he'd had a knife, it would have been all over. No matter how hard you trained, if you weren't expecting a fist, it was going to come at you and take you by surprise.

'Don't you make a sound now, Chaz,' the man said from behind the mask. 'If you do, you won't be seeing your boyfriend again. Do as I ask and I'll let you go. Eventually. I need you just now and you're going to help me. I can do it with you dead or alive. The choice is yours. Understand?'

His eyes weren't piercing, more like bloodshot from too much drink and not enough sleep. His breath was pungent, like he only had a distant relationship with a toothbrush.

She nodded and looked him up and down. Dressed in black, heavy overcoat with the hoody underneath, and the ski mask. It was coming down so hard with snow that nobody would pay him any attention.

'Don't even think about it. Do you fucking understand?'

'Yes.'

'Right, give me your phone.'

She handed it over and he put it in his pocket. 'Will you be seeing your boyfriend in the morning?'

'He's not my boyfriend. We're colleagues.'

'Sure you are. Answer me.'

'No, I won't be seeing him then.'

'Get through to the bathroom and get cleaned up. And I'll be watching.'

He marched her through and watched as she staunched the bleeding with a towel.

'Get changed. You're not going out like that.'

'And you're going to watch?'

'Yes. Don't worry, I've seen better.'

She tutted and took a clean blouse out of her wardrobe and changed into it.

'Get your coat on. We're going for a drive.' She put her thick coat on.

'Before we go...' He brought out a set of handcuffs and slapped one cuff on her wrist and the other on his own wrist. 'When we get outside, you're not going to scream. If you do, I will leave you behind, but I won't have time to unlock the cuffs. I'll stomp on your hand until all the bones are broken, then I'll slide it off your wrist. It will be broken so badly they'll have to amputate it. The choice is yours: come quietly and we'll have a nice drive, or start shouting like a wee girl and lose your hand.'

'Who are you?' she asked.

'That's not important. If you see me, I'll have to kill you. In the car, I'll remove my mask and the cuffs. You won't look at me. If you do, I will make a call to my colleague and he will kill your brother, Roger. Understand?'

'Leave my brother alone.'

'Again, this is all in your hands. I just need help with something and then it's all over. You can come back to your normal life.' He stared at her. 'You going to come quietly?'

'Yes. Please just leave Roger alone.'

'Nobody's touched him. Yet.'

They went out into the dark and the snow and didn't see anybody. They reached a van, and he opened the back door and got her to step in, taking his cuffed hand with her.

When she was looking the other way, she felt something sting her neck and then...darkness.

Now, here she was, in a cold, dark room, with only the sounds of the wind outside and a child crying softly. Never one to feed her imagination, she broke her own rule now.

And realised she was fucked.

THIRTY-ONE

'Wallis isn't his last name, it's his middle name. Peter Wallis Connolly. That's his full name. Wallis after my dad. Peter after *his* dad.' She nodded to McDonald.

'He's your son?' Bracken said.

'Yes. Stuart and I met at university and we had a love affair. I got pregnant and we both agreed it wouldn't be in our best interests to keep the baby. He would be better off with a family who could show him love and bring him up well. I was only twenty, Stuart was twenty-two. Peter was given up for adoption.'

McDonald looked at Bracken. 'I met Natalie later on in life and she's almost ten years younger than me. We didn't think we were going to have any kids, so we stopped trying, and that's when she fell pregnant with Rory. I was over the moon. He means the world to me.

Natalie did too, but she did that stupid stuff with the drugs. I took Rory away for his own good.'

'And married a much younger woman. Who was carrying your child,' Bracken said. 'Where can we get hold of Peter?'

'I don't know,' Ailsa said. 'If I knew, I would tell you.'

'Why has he come back now?'

She looked him in the eyes. 'He came back six years ago, remember? I told you I didn't kill those kids. I think Peter did. He contacted me, but I didn't want to see him. He left. I didn't think I would ever hear from him again.'

'And did you?' Bracken asked.

'No. But then Robert got a new patient, a young man who was acting weird. Even for somebody who needs therapy, I mean. Robert had an uneasy feeling about him, but didn't think much more about it. He was still the force psychologist and had plenty of work. Your friend Bob Long for a start. As part of his medical retirement, the force still sends him along, trying to help him. He used to talk about me a lot to Robert, not knowing Robert and I were conducting a relationship of sorts.'

'And Robert told you what they spoke about?' Bracken said.

'Unethical, I know, but yes. And he told me what this young man was saying. Because he too brought up my name.'

'What name did he go by?'

She shrugged. 'Peter Wallis. I assume he thought he didn't have to hide it from Robert.'

'Any idea what his adopted name is?'

'No. We were never told,' McDonald said.

Then Bracken's phone rang. He took it out of his pocket and saw it was a FaceTime call. He answered it.

'Chaz. I'm sort of busy at the moment.' Then the phone was brought more towards her face and he could see she had been crying. When it was taken away again, he saw the knife being held at her throat.

He froze for a second, then quickly composed himself. With the hand that was out of sight, he waved McDonald over; then, when the man was almost beside him, he put up a hand to tell him to stop. McDonald could see the screen, but the caller couldn't see him.

'What's going on?' Bracken asked.

'He took me last night. Brought me somewhere and told me to talk to you. You have to listen or he's going to kill us.'

'Us?'

Her eyes looked off to one side before looking back

at him. She was in a dark room and only the light from the phone was illuminating her face.

'Yes. Me, Rory and Robert.'

THIRTY-TWO

The room was silent as they looked at the phone screen, only Bracken's face showing.

Chaz cleared her throat before speaking again. 'He says he knows the procedure. That armed teams will be sent here. He said to tell you that he wants Ailsa Connolly to come here in exchange for the three of us. He will be looking out for her coming, and if there are any firearms teams, we will die before they get to us.'

'Where are you?' Bracken asked.

She looked off camera for a moment and Bracken could hear somebody talking in a very low voice, but he couldn't make out the words.

'He was expecting you go and see Ailsa after discovering her husband was gone. He can see you're in the hospital now. Is he correct?'

Bracken looked at both McDonald and Ailsa, and they nodded.

'Yes, I'm here.'

'Right. He says he wants Ailsa to go to the place where she lived with her family when she was a small girl.'

'Which is where?'

'Starvation Lake.'

Bracken looked puzzled and looked at Ailsa.

'The small house we lived in up north was on the banks of Loch Srath nan Sarbhaidh. I couldn't pronounce it, so my dad called it Starvation Lake. I haven't been there in years.'

Chaz spoke again. 'He wants me to remind you that he knows exactly how the police will think. How they operate. Since he was a police officer himself. He wants Bracken and Ailsa to come along alone. With Stuart McDonald. Bracken will take us away while he gets to keep Ailsa and McDonald. A fair swap, he says.'

'First of all,' Bracken said, 'they're not going to allow Ailsa to walk out of here with me. That's not a reasonable request.'

They heard a scream off camera and Chaz whipped her head round. 'You fucking leave him alone!' she screamed, bucking against the chair she was tied to. They heard a slap and her head snapped back again. Blood was coming out of the corner of her mouth.

'He just grabbed Rory's ear and twisted it. He says that Rory's dad can make anything happen. It's either this or Rory goes into the lake with rocks tied to his ankles. I'm sorry, Sean.' She started crying again, but then her head was pulled back by the hair. She squealed.

'Let her go and I'll bring Ailsa,' Bracken said.

Suddenly, Chaz's hair was released and her head moved sharply forward.

She listened again, then faced the camera. 'You have until ten tonight. Twelve hours. Enough time to get things organised and get up here. It's a long drive, he says. Only you, McDonald and Ailsa are to come or else we all die.'

'I'm going to get it organised now. I'll call you back.'

'He says not to hang up –' she started to say, but Bracken cut the call. He didn't want to hand all the power to whoever was holding them.

'What the bloody hell do we do now?' McDonald asked.

'Do you have the power to release her?' Bracken asked him.

'Well, yes. There's procedure of course, a lot of paperwork, but ultimately it's my decision.'

'We don't have time for paperwork and the decision was already made for you.'

McDonald nodded. 'I'll have my secretary draw up the emergency release papers. I'll sign them later.'

'Do that.'

'Meantime, you can have a platoon of armed police get up there.'

Bracken looked at him. 'Didn't you hear him?'

'I don't give a shit. I want him captured.'

Bracken stepped closer to him. 'We'll be lucky if they're not dead within the hour. Or certainly when we say we're coming, there's a fifty-fifty chance of him killing them.'

'Oh my God,' McDonald said, wiping a hand over his face. 'What the hell do we do?'

'I think I know who's behind this.'

'We know who's behind it, Sean,' Ailsa said. 'It's our son.'

'You heard what Chaz said: he told her he was a police officer,' Bracken pointed out. He thought back to what his friend had said about how much he hated Ailsa. He would do anything to get his hands on her for revenge.

'I think it's my old friend Bob Long, the man who owns the guest house I'm staying at.'

'What makes you say that?' McDonald said.

Bracken looked at Ailsa before speaking. 'He

blames Ailsa for what happened to him. He tried to rescue two little boys from a fire, not knowing they were already dead. He broke his back and was pensioned out of the force. He's bitter and twisted about it.'

'Good God. And he fucking took my little boy? By Christ, I want us to go to this place, Bracken, this Starvation Lake.' McDonald turned to Ailsa. 'Where the hell is it?'

'North Perthshire. It's so isolated. Up the A9 to Craigallan. It's a small village in the middle of nowhere, on the edge of the loch. We lived there when I was a little girl. The village's lifeblood is the Craigallan distillery. It still is, I believe.'

'How long would it take to drive there?' Bracken asked.

'An hour and a half. But in this weather? God knows. It will be treacherous.'

'They fucking made it,' McDonald said.

'That was before the storm that's coming in. It's already hit the coast. A big one,' Bracken said. 'We'd have to move now.'

McDonald was already on the phone talking to somebody. He hung up and turned to an orderly. 'Take me to a computer.'

The man hesitated.

'Now!'

That got him moving and he left with McDonald, leaving Bracken and Ailsa alone.

'You could have told me this yesterday. We could have been looking for him.'

'I'm sorry. I thought you were going to try to railroad Robert, try to rope him in and charge him for the murders of those women. I was wrong.'

'I'm not pointing the finger. But tell me, do you think Peter killed those kids years ago and tried to blame you?'

She lowered her eyes, like she was ashamed, then she looked up at him. 'Yes. I do. I didn't then, of course, but knowing what we know now, I have no doubt.'

'It all makes sense. I think Bob Long has been observing you from the outside, watching you and Robert. He goes to Robert for therapy, and I'm not sure if he found out about your son or not, but these three murders have tipped him over the edge. He needs to blame somebody for them and he's blaming you.'

'Killing me isn't going to stop Peter. Peter will carry on killing.'

'You and I know that, but Bob is unstable so we know he isn't thinking straight.'

McDonald came back into the room holding a piece of paper. 'I got my secretary to email me a copy of the emergency release form. I've signed it and I'll take a photo and send it back to her.' He looked at Ailsa.

'For the time being, you're a free woman. Released into mine and Bracken's custody. You've been doing well, Ailsa, but if you fuck this up, I'll have your arse transferred right back to Carstairs. You understand?'

'Of course.'

'Then let's go.'

'Wait,' said Bracken. 'I know he says we need to go up there just the three of us, but I think that's foolish. I think we should take a couple of members from my team.'

'He'll kill the hostages if he sees them.'

'We'll go in separate cars. We'll get a police escort up the road, go as fast as we can to beat the weather, then my team can hang back and give us backup.'

'How long will it take them to meet us?'

'They're just around the corner. At Robert's house.'

'Call them. We need to go now. I don't want to get up there and be poncing about in the dark.'

Bracken made the call.

THIRTY-THREE

McDonald and Ailsa were sitting in Bracken's car. In the car behind them were Sullivan and Nelson. In front and behind were two high-speed pursuit cars, lights flashing, waiting to take off.

'Right, Jimmy, we're off. Nelson? Make sure that Angie and Izzie stay in the incident room.'

'Yes, sir.'

Bracken stood up straight and tapped the roof before going to his own car. He got in and looked in the mirror. 'You like rollercoasters? They're fuck all compared to how we're going to be driving.'

'I don't care, just get my boy back,' McDonald said, but buckled up anyway. No point in tempting fate, especially when your life was in the hands of somebody else.

Bracken honked the horn and the lead patrol car

took off, with Bracken right on its heels. The snow was starting to get heavier, but he had never been so focused in his life. They left Morningside, with other patrol cars creating a corridor for them to sail through, and they had outriders buzzing around them, keeping junctions clear.

Bracken turned the heat down, his eyes on the lead car all the way. It took fifteen minutes to reach Queensferry Road, where the speed started in earnest, despite the snow getting heavier.

They had to slow down the further north they got, as the snow was thicker here and the traffic slower.

'This is painful,' McDonald said. 'I'm going to punch that bastard right in the mouth, copper or no copper.'

'I think his retirement from the force just ended,' Bracken replied. 'Kidnapping and killing people tend to do that for your pension. Where he's going, he won't need it.'

Ailsa sat quietly, holding McDonald's hand.

Just north of Dunkeld, they took the slip road and the lead patrol car pulled in at the side of the road. Bracken pulled up alongside it and wound the passenger window down. 'Good job, ladies. Thanks for getting us here as fast as you did.'

The female sergeant nodded to him. 'Thank you, sir.'

'You know what's happening next, yes?'

'Yes, sir.'

Bracken grinned as he wound the window back up. 'Over to you, Ailsa. This is your country we're in now.'

'Left at the roundabout.'

Bracken pulled away and saw Sullivan following him, the second escort car staying behind the first.

This was a narrower road and Bracken had to balance getting there fast and getting there alive.

'How long?' he asked.

'About half an hour with sunshine and low traffic. Longer than that since it looks like we're in the Arctic Circle.'

'Christ.' It was early afternoon, but as the clouds threw down every piece of snow they had, and seemingly in one go, it could have been any time. There was a car in front going slowly, too slowly for Bracken, so he indicated and put his foot down, overtaking.

He couldn't see the driver, but if he were a betting man, he'd have said it was an old man, barely tall enough to see over the steering wheel and old enough to think that he was about to go and join his mother and father up above.

Sullivan was right on Bracken's tail, in a bout of 'fuck it all' driving. Bracken was starting to like the man. Unlike Charlie Nelson, who was too much of a clown.

The road was starting to get covered when they passed through a little town.

'The next one is ours,' Ailsa said, and she looked pale. Bracken couldn't blame her.

Twenty minutes later, they entered the small village of Craigallan, home of the famous Craigallan single malt. Bracken had tasted the whisky many times before and was impressed.

The road veered round to the right, but Ailsa leaned forward and said, 'Go straight, towards the marina. It's near there.'

Marina? Bracken wondered. He couldn't even see the fucking loch for the snow.

He indicated and pulled into the car park opposite the small marina. He was sweating with the heat on, but knew his face would be ripped off by the extreme cold if he opened the window.

Sullivan pulled in behind him.

Bracken turned off the engine and got out, taking the keys with him. That was all he needed, this turning out to be a huge hoax and Ailsa fucking off with the car.

Sullivan wound his window down. He was smiling. 'Jesus, I've never driven like that before. Never been called a mad bastard by Nelson before either, but in all honesty he could have been talking about you.'

'A wing and a prayer, son, that's what got us here. But listen, that cottage is here. I'd like to go in on foot.'

'Gotcha.'

Bracken turned back to his own car and saw Ailsa standing outside.

'Christ, she could do a runner, boss.'

'Hardly. I just handcuffed her to the headrest.'

'Headrests can be taken out.'

'Nobody likes a smartarse, Jimmy.' He turned and walked back through the deepening snow to the car, narrowing his eyes against the driving snow.

He reached Ailsa, whose hair was getting covered in snow. 'Look. Up there,' she said. 'The new houses they're building.'

'What about them?' Bracken asked.

She looked at him. 'That's where our old house used to be.'

THIRTY-FOUR

'Jesus, do you think they were in Edinburgh and we've been played?' Stuart McDonald said as he got out of the car.

Bracken didn't have the answer. Yet.

Sullivan and Nelson got out of their car and joined them.

'They're building houses on the site of Ailsa's old home.' Bracken looked at Sullivan. 'Not right at this minute, obviously.'

'What now? You think they got us out of Edinburgh just to get us out of the way?'

'God knows.' Bracken looked at Ailsa again, studying her features. She looked older than she had just six short years ago, with more lines round her eyes. Could she be that cunning? Had she planned this with McDonald?

Then he thought of Robert, the mild-mannered man she had married. Chalk and cheese. Why would she have married him? His gut told him she wasn't controlling this.

'The church,' she said, turning to look at Bracken, her arm still in the car. He reached in and took the handcuffs off. He was rewarded with a small, sad smile.

'Church?' he said.

'When we had a drink, all those years ago, didn't you listen to a word I said? About my past?'

'Now I wish I had. Might not be getting a tongue-lashing now if I had.'

'Seriously. I told you my father was a minister and had his own parish. It was here. That's why we lived here, in the little house. It's why I now want to follow in his footsteps.'

'Where is this church?' McDonald asked.

She turned to the marina and nodded over the loch. 'Over on the other side. It's a small church built on a little outcrop. It has a great view of the loch. It's empty now, since they built the new one.'

'Does Robert know about it?' Bracken asked.

'Yes, of course. He knows everything there is to know about me. He listened to me when I told him.'

He turned to Sullivan. 'We need to get across there. If they aren't there then we've been had.'

They got back in the cars and went through the

village, waiting at the red light to cross over the single-track bridge. Tree-covered hills rose in the distance, painted white with snow, but the peaks disappeared into the snow-laden clouds.

The road took them to the other side of the village.

'It's around the bend, on the left. You can't miss it.'

But Bracken did miss it, on purpose. He wanted to see if there were any vehicles parked outside and there was, an old van. An old stone barn was on the opposite side of the road and Bracken put his indicator on and turned into its driveway, the snow thick here and getting thicker. The car slid sideways for a moment and he thought he was going to get stuck, but the car soldiered on and he stopped.

Sullivan pulled up alongside, his car sliding dangerously close for a moment before he corrected it.

'Jimmy, you and Nelson leave your car here. The church can't be seen from here, so I assume they can't see us. See if you can get over there on foot.'

'Okay. What are you going to do?'

'I'm just going to drive over and fucking march right in.'

THIRTY-FIVE

Maybe it was the anger he was barely controlling, maybe it was just the thought of whoever it was holding a knife to a woman's throat and abducting a helpless wee boy, but Bracken drove the car fast into the church car park and licked the brakes on. The car skidded through the snow and he thought at first that it was going to carry on and knock the front door off its hinges, but they glided to a halt.

He turned the engine off and turned to McDonald. 'Can you fight?'

McDonald looked unsure for a moment. 'Well, I don't go brawling in pubs if that's what you mean.'

'I mean, if some bastard in there is going to give you a tanking then kill your boy, can you step up and have a fucking go?'

'Of course I can. Can you?'

Bracken smiled, but it was full of malice. 'You'd better fucking believe I can. Let's go.' He opened his door and stepped out into the driving snow, which was being whipped up by a vicious wind.

Ailsa and McDonald were right behind him, and at that moment in time he couldn't have cared less if the pair of them fucked off. The man he wanted was inside this church and by God he wasn't leaving a free man.

Bracken walked up to the door, noticing the pair following him. He opened it and walked into the cold of the old church. It was clear it wasn't used anymore, except maybe to hold people hostage.

He saw the two heads in the front pew, facing the front, and something sucked the breath from him.

They didn't look round.

He thought they were dead, propped up like deceased Victorian relatives waiting to have their final photograph taken.

It was clear Bob Long wasn't dead. He was at the pulpit, staring at Bracken.

'Those who are without sin cast the first stone! Are there any of us here who haven't broken the law in some way? I don't think so! You are all responsible for this!'

Then he locked eyes with Ailsa Connolly. 'And here she is, the lady of the hour! Welcome. Walk forward so we can see you.'

Bracken turned to look at Ailsa. 'You don't have to do this.'

'Yes, I do, Sean.' She walked forward, Bracken and McDonald following. Chaz and Robert instinctively turned around to look even though they were blindfolded. They also had gags in their mouths.

'Sean!' Bob shouted, but it was too late. The church door slammed shut and Bracken turned to look with the others at the killer who was holding Rory McDonald.

'Hello, Sean.'

Billy Burton was holding a knife to Rory's neck.

'I'm sorry, Sean,' Bob Long said. 'That fucker said he would kill us all if I didn't do as he said. He's a mad bastard.'

'Shut up, Bob! Stop that bloody whining!' Burton said.

Bracken tried to keep the surprise off his face. 'Come on, Billy. Why are you doing this?'

'It's her I want. These other people are just pawns in a game. You can all go, if you like. But you're not taking her back.'

Bracken held out his hands and took a step forward. Burton yanked on the boy's hair and pressed the knife closer to his throat.

'I've been at this game a lot longer than you. I know the drill. The soft voice, the hands up in the air. All the tricks in the book. But you know I'm not here for a laugh. I want revenge on Ailsa Connolly for killing my grandchildren and their mother. And their father, my son.'

'I didn't kill the children,' Ailsa said. 'It was somebody else.'

'Of course it was. It was never you, was it?! You're saying that so McDonald can let you go into the care of the community, something that wouldn't happen if you admitted to killing those kids.'

'She's right, Billy. Listen to her.' Bracken took a step closer. 'Let the boy go. He's done nothing to you.'

'I'm just using him to get to her. And him!' Burton nodded towards McDonald. 'Can't you see what she did, Bracken? She killed those innocent grandchildren of mine, took my whole family away from me. I couldn't see her walking the streets again.'

'Where is he, Billy?' Bracken said.

'Where's who?'

Bracken made eye contact with him. 'Peter Wallis. The man we're looking for. Your accomplice.'

Burton laughed. 'How do you know I've got an accomplice?'

'Aw, come on!' Bracken raised his voice, the sound booming around the small church.

Bob Long had walked round from the pulpit, sat

down beside Chaz and pulled off her blindfold and gag. He got her to move round and untied her wrists.

'Help Robert,' Bob whispered, and she nodded and began untying Marshall.

'It was me! I killed them!' Burton shouted. 'To get back at McDonald!'

Bracken got closer. 'No, you didn't. We have a witness, remember? The woman who showed Peter Wallis round the house, the one with the garage you fucking stood in on Saturday looking down at the corpse of Maggie Scott. Do you think we'll believe it was some old bastard like you?'

'You watch your fucking mouth, Bracken. I killed those women.'

'Jesus, are you not going to admit it was Ailsa's son? We know all about him.'

The air seemed to go out of Burton. 'Well, I would have done it, but he wanted to.'

'Why, Billy?'

'When I saw your application for a transfer, I needed to act fast. I knew she was heading for release sooner rather than later, and I wanted you to realise she was still a murdering cow, whether she did it with her own hand or had her son do it.'

'You knew I had a son?' Ailsa said.

'Thanks to your husband. I was in therapy with him, just like Bob there. Just like your son was. I overheard him one day, by accident, telling Robert who he was. I put two and two together and figured out he had just as big a beef with you as I had. He hates you more than I do.'

'Where is he?'

'I have no idea.'

Bracken turned to Marshall. 'Who is he?'

'He just told me he was Ailsa's son. I know him as Peter Wallis.'

'And you didn't tell me?' Ailsa asked him.

'I'm sorry, love,' said Marshall. 'I didn't know how to. I share things with you, but I just couldn't get my head around that. He told me he was working up the courage to talk to you and I was helping him. He wanted it to be a surprise.'

'Mission accomplished,' Bracken said. Then to Burton, 'Tell us where he is.'

'I don't know. His job is done. Mine is to finish Ailsa off. Nobody else needs to get hurt. Give her to me, you get the boy and we leave. That's it.'

'Oh, come on, Billy, you know it doesn't work that way. I won't insult your intelligence by telling you otherwise.'

'You can make it happen.' Burton pulled the boy in closer. 'Get over here, Ailsa.'

She stepped forward. Bracken put a hand out, but

she brushed it away. 'No, Sean. This boy's life is worth more than mine. If he wants me, he can take me.'

She walked forward, and at that moment Burton pushed Rory away and grabbed hold of Ailsa.

He smiled. 'Now you're talking sense. I lied. I know where your son is and he's going to meet me. I'm going to take you to your son, and he'll deal with you.'

He was about to turn around when the door to the church opened and Peter Wallis walked in.

THIRTY-SIX

'What the fuck are you doing here? It's almost over.'

'It *is* over, Billy,' Charlie Nelson said. He brought the knife out from behind his back and rammed it into Burton's back. The older detective gasped and let go of Ailsa.

Nelson grabbed hold of her. 'Let's go. You and me. I'm not going to hurt you. I just want you back.'

'Did you kill those children back then?'

'Of course I did, Mum. I was emulating you. I wanted to be just like you. Burton and Bracken started to get suspicious. I heard them talking. I was trying to get them off your back, but it didn't work.'

'You killed children, Peter.'

'Charlie, remember? Charlie Nelson. That's the name they gave me when you gave me away. I just wanted to be with you again. Burton spoke to me. He knew who I was after he overheard your husband talking to me. He said there was a way for us to be together again. I just had to kill those women and they would release you. They would see you were innocent. But he took the little boy. He was doing this all for himself, to get back at you. That's not what he told me he was doing. It was all supposed to be about me and you getting back with each other.'

'Peter, listen, son. You can't be doing this. How would all of this work?'

Charlie Nelson might have been oblivious to the blue flashing lights coming in through the stained-glass windows, but Ailsa wasn't.

'You need help, son. Isn't that why you went to Robert in the first place?'

'Yes! I knew who you were. What you were doing. I've been keeping tabs on you for years. And I was doing fine until Burton got inside my head! I thought I could fight for you from the inside by putting doubt in their minds. It was working. Then he messed everything up. We have to go, Mum. We have to go now.'

'You're going fucking nowhere,' Bracken said.

'Really? You want to do this, Mr Hero? Then let's fucking dance.'

Nelson roughly pushed his mother aside and drew his hand back. Maybe for a brief second he thought he had an extendable baton in his hand instead of a knife, but drawing his hand back gave Bracken a precious few seconds.

He stepped forward and grabbed Nelson's arm as it made the downward swing, head-butted him, put his right leg behind Nelson's and took him down. He drew back a fist, but Ailsa shouted at him as she kicked away the fallen knife.

He stopped and turned Nelson over, careful not to get blood on himself from Nelson's bleeding face.

'You bastard!' McDonald said, coming over. 'I'll see you're fucking put away in Carstairs for the rest of your fucking life.'

Bracken cuffed Nelson just as the female sergeant came rushing in ahead of the other uniforms. 'We got stuck behind a slow truck, sir,' she said.

'This is DC Charlie Nelson. You might know him. He's our serial killer. Get him on his feet.' Bracken read him his rights and let the uniformed crew take over.

He turned to look for Ailsa and saw only Bob, Chaz and McDonald with his son. 'Where're Ailsa and Robert?' he asked.

'There's another door round here at the side,' Chaz said. 'It's open.'

'Oh, Christ. She's gone.'

Bracken ran outside and saw Robert standing with an arm around Ailsa by a patrol car.

Ailsa looked at Bracken. 'If I want to eventually get

out, I want it done the right way,' she said, and they both got in the police car.

Bracken looked over to an ambulance, where Jimmy Sullivan was sitting. The snow was still coming down hard as he walked over.

'The bastard clocked me with a log or something. I went down like a sack of potatoes. Sorry, boss. I'll put in for a transfer from MIT tomorrow.'

'We're going to be stuck here overnight. Just you concentrate on getting treated and never mind a bloody transfer.'

'Thanks, sir.'

'Useless bastard.' He smiled at Sullivan and turned back to the church. Chaz was standing in the doorway. He walked over to her.

'Well, you did say you would get me into a church one day,' he said to her.

'No, I didn't.'

'Maybe not, but you were thinking it.'

'Yeah, so I was.' She smiled at him and kissed him on the cheek. 'Thank you for coming here in time.'

'Sir Galahad, that's me.'

Bob Long walked up behind her. 'Hey, Sean.'

'Hi, pal. How you doing?'

'Better now. I don't know if it was being in church or hearing Nelson confess, but I feel a weight has been lifted off my shoulders.'

'Maybe you can put this bitterness behind you now, Bob.' Bracken looked at them both. 'Come on, we've still got a lot to sort out. Finding somewhere to spend the night for one thing.'

'Aren't you a fast worker, Bracken?' Chaz said.

'We're just colleagues, remember?'

'Keep telling yourself that.'

THIRTY-SEVEN

Christmas Eve

'Who the hell are you?' said the man in the chair. He was sweating, a thin bead of sweat running along his forehead. It could be seen in the very dimly lit room.

'Let's just say I'm a friend of a friend.'

'What do you want?' He looked at Bracken, aware of two other men behind him.

The old farmhouse was deserted and nobody had been here for a long time. It had been a struggle to get the car up here, but the four-wheel drive system had coped well.

Bracken noted that the grave of Ailsa Connolly's sixth victim had been filled in a long time ago and nobody would ever know it had been there.

'This is how it's going to go down. You're going to transfer whatever money you stole from your parents back into the joint bank account you still have. The money you got from the sale of their house too. They have a new power of attorney: me.'

'Oh, I see, you want the money for yourself? You're a conman.'

Bracken walked right up to him. 'Roddy, I am only going to say this once. I am going to help your parents. I am not going to take one penny from them. Ever. You're going to give them their money back, just what was rightfully theirs. Then you're going to fuck off down south to live.'

'And if I don't want to do that?'

'Then we'll just walk out of here and you'll never see us again.'

'Really? Just like that.'

'Just like that. But see those men in the shadows? Oh wait, you can't. Well, they see you and they know everything there is to know about you. You walk out of here and one day they'll meet you again. Only this time, you'll never see it coming.'

Roddy's phone was on a small table in front of him, light shining down on it from a small storm lantern. Never much of a fighter, Roddy grabbed his phone and transferred the money from his own account into his parent's account.

'Good job. Now, after Christmas I will go with them to the bank. They will open a new account without your name on it and transfer the funds over. These men behind you will be watching you every minute. If I find out you've gone back and there are no funds there, you'll wish you had never met me.'

'I already wish that.'

'Go live your life, Roddy, and stop fucking people over, especially your parents.'

Roddy nodded.

'There's a bus stop down at the foot of the track. You can walk down, or we can put the hood back on and these men will put you in the boot of the car again.'

'I'll walk, I'll walk.' He watched as Bracken took a knife out from behind his back. 'God, no, please!' he shouted.

Bracken merely stabbed the knife into the table. 'Cut the ropes tying your legs to the chair. Wait ten minutes, then leave.'

'What time's the bus?'

'Don't push your luck.'

THIRTY-EIGHT

'Merry Christmas!' Mary said, sitting down. The turkey was in the middle of the table and the trimmings were in bowls. 'If nobody minds, I'd like to ask Sean to carve the bird this year?'

Bob Long cheered and clapped. They were all wearing party hats. Natalie sat beside Rory, trying to make Christmas as normal as possible for him. Stuart McDonald had popped round that morning to drop some gifts off, before heading back to his parents', where he was staying. His house would be put on the market very soon.

Billy Burton's funeral would be after Christmas, and private, and Charlie Nelson was in custody, but nobody mentioned them.

Mr and Mrs Clark were smiling. Chaz was sitting

beside Bracken, and she squeezed his hand before he stood up.

'It would be my pleasure,' he said, and took the carving knife and cut into the turkey.

Mr Clark opened an envelope that had his name on the front. 'It's a note. "Check your bank account." I think Roddy had a change of heart.' He looked at his wife. 'Who else would have brought this?'

They both looked at Sean.

'Santa Claus,' Bracken said, and smiled at Chaz. 'Merry Christmas, everybody.'

AFTERWORD

Another detective novel set in Edinburgh, John? I hear you ask. Well, settle down and let me explain.

Before Frank Miller, before Harry McNeil, there was Sean Bracken. He was created way back in the 1990's.

My character was married, had a son and daughter, and his son was a uniformed police officer. He ended up divorced and moved in with a pathologist. I sent the book out to agents and although it got good reception, it wasn't picked up. So I went back to the drawing board and created a new detective.

I made him younger, his wife was dead, his father lived with him. He was a successful cop and then a young woman came into his life. I called him Frank Miller.

Long story short, years later, I self-published

Miller, and I used some of the elements from Bracken in those books, like a detective moving in with a pathologist. Then I created Harry McNeil, and again, used some elements from the Bracken novel, like having Harry's son in a police officer's uniform.

Fast forward to a year ago. I wanted a dedicated office built in my basement, but it was going to take some time and co-ordination to get things going. Including tidying out some of the junk we'd acquired before I could get a contractor in. I was busy writing, and slowly going through stuff in my office, and I came across some Bracken notes. So I had an idea. What if I could take this book, and re-write it from the ground up, but keep the main plot and characters? Would it work? I thought I would take a chance and wrote the first few chapters while writing Harry McNeil.

And this is the end result. That's why I have three Edinburgh detective series going. Will Frank Miller return? Only time will tell. Harry McNeil certainly will. And Bracken? He's up next in book two, titled *Think Twice*. Coming at the end of January 2021. Will he appear after that? I think so. I enjoyed revisiting him.

Before that though, Harry McNeil will appear on New Year's Eve 2020, in *Rush to Judgement*.

Now I would like to thank some people for helping me. Ruth, a police officer from Police Scotland who took the time to answer my questions. All my advance readers, who are a terrific bunch. I'd love to get together with them all one day. A huge thank you to Kara Page, for going above and beyond. To Sylvia. To my daughters for always believing in me. And to my wife, Debbie, who does the important job of entertaining the dogs.

Last but not least, to my readers, the ones who make this all possible. If you have a spare couple of minutes, could I ask you to please leave a review or a rating on Amazon or Goodreads? Every single one is truly appreciated. Thank you in advance.

In this uncertain time, stay safe my friends. All the best.

John Carson
    New York
    November 2020

Printed in Great Britain
by Amazon